THE INGREDIENTS IN THIS BOOK INCLUDE:

PASTRAMI QUEENS
TWO-HEADED COWS
A DRUG CALLED "PLOTZ"
TOILET MUSEUMS
WEREWOLF HAIRSTYLISTS
COLONEL SANDERS
VIOLENT BAR MITZVAHS
LION ALLERGIES
THE RIVER STYX
SUPERHEROINE WEAPONRY
KABBALAH-SAVVY ROCK STARS
LUCIFER ON A BEACH
GHOSTLY GRAFFITI
KIDNAP INSURANCE
JESUS DOING LAUNDRY
A BUENOS AIRES SHOOTOUT
OBSESSIVE TWINS
DILLINGER REINCARNATED
MILLION-DOLLAR BILLS
BAD LUCK WITH SAMOYEDS
ETHIOPIAN NAZI HUNTERS
A HOUSE MADE OF PASTA
BELLY BUTTON EXPERIMENTS
DUCHAMP'S SUITCASE
THE LIVES OF PIRATES
SOAP NOSTALGIA
ACTUARY SIDEKICKS
THE AMISH IN LAS VEGAS
VENGEFUL ELEPHANTS
YOGI BERRA
TERRORISTS IN DRAG
BULLFIGHT COMEUPPANCE
ALCHEMISTS' LAUGHTER
GORILLAS IN TAXICABS
REVERSE VOYEURISM
UNAVENGED COUSIN-KILLERS
WOMEN NAMED "ETHEL"
THE WORD "FUCK"
TIME-TRAVELING CONQUISTADORS
A UNIQUE AVALANCHE RESCUE TECHNIQUE
THE SANTA BARBARA COUNTY DRUNK TANK
A CULT CALLED "GASTROLOGOS"
A SEX WORKER CALLED "GRANDMA"
and
PEARL BAILEY SINGING "SEVENTY-SIX TROMBONES"

WE LOVED THE WORLD BUT COULD NOT STAY

GARY LIPPMAN

WE LOVED THE WORLD BUT COULD NOT STAY

GARY LIPPMAN

RARE BIRD
LOS ANGELES, CALIF.

THIS IS A GENUINE RARE BIRD BOOK

Rare Bird Books
6044 North Figueroa Street
Los Angeles, CA 90042
rarebirdbooks.com

Set in Warnock
Printed in the United States

10 9 8 7 6 5 4 3 2 1

Library of Congress Cataloging-in-Publication Data available upon request.

For Verka,

For my three guys,
Billy, Buddy, and Gabou,

and

For Ettie Pearl, The HQ,
with love and DB

Out with the truckers and the kickers and the cowboy angels
And a good saloon in every single town
Oh, but I remembered something you once told me
And I'll be damned if it did not come true
Twenty thousand roads I went down, down, down
And they all led me straight back home to you.

—Gram Parsons and Tom S. Brown,
"The Return of the Grievous Angel"

since feeling is first
who pays any attention
to the syntax of things
will never wholly kiss you;
wholly to be a fool
while Spring is in the world
my blood approves,
and kisses are a better fate
than wisdom

—ee cummings
"since feeling is first"

I wish I could just say everything in one word. I hate all the things
that can happen between the beginning of a sentence and the end.

—Leonard Cohen

MOONBURN

You woke to find the full moon on your cheek, neatly balanced as if it belonged there, but you mistook it for a pimple, and you popped it.

WHOLE LOTTA PASTA GOIN' ON

"Merlin," I said, "please help, I was a fool and sold my house, my happy childhood home, and now the town council plans to tear it down tomorrow," and after thrusting his beard into his mouth and munching it fiercely, the wizard said, "I have no influence over town councils, but I *do* have an idea," and so he changed my Camelot into a giant chunk of pasta—*al dente*, how I like it—and I was swallowing the last bite just as the bulldozer came rumbling up Oak Crest Road.

ROOM 48 IN THE HEART OF AUTUMN

Although he'd loved her for all the time he'd known her, the master *origami* artist shed no tears for his wife until five weeks after her death, when he compared an ear of rice to his rendering of it and saw no difference between the two and for a moment felt like God before recalling how weak he was with everything except for paper.

FEET

As a lover of feet—shapely ones, for the most part, but *any* tootsies were capable of giving him a tingle—Map assumed that his new job as a salesperson in a shoe store would be nonstop bliss, but soon enough he discovered the wisdom of the Austrian journalist Karl Kraus, who said, "The tragedy of the foot fetishist is that he must spend time with the person attached to the foot."

I'M YOUNG BUT YOU LOOK ME OLD

Next to a sign reading *"Public Writer"* at a chipped wooden desk in the main post office of Saigon (Pryna refused to call it "Ho Chi Minh City" because her POW father died in one of Ho's prisons), a wizened man has been working for sixty years, outlasting the rampage of local history while translating his customers' letters (English, French, Vietnamese—he speaks all three), and the night after Pryna met him, she drank Hadacol in her hotel room and fell asleep and heard a voice, her father's voice, saying, "For as long as that Public Writer lives, we'll know and understand each other, but the moment he breathes his last, this world will shatter into gibberish and strife."

WHAT THE WORD "FUCK" MEANS

"Did you know that the word *'fuck'* is a curse?" said the boy with the Batman lunchbox in our cafeteria on the first day of first grade, and because I thought he meant a *witch's* curse, which seemed intriguing, I went to confirm it with our teacher, a brutal woman named Mrs. Schultz, but because Schultz seemed to dislike hearing the word "fuck" spoken, at least by a child, she smacked me across the face and knocked me down, which made everyone (including that Batman-lunchbox boy) burst into laughter, and because I didn't want to let them see me cry, I bit my lip and held it all in until I got home and my mother said, "How was school?" at which point I let go, filling our house with so many tears that when a plumber eventually showed up, water-pump in hand, he looked at the knee-deep flood I'd caused and said, "What the *fuck*?"

I'LL FLY AWAY

At a party in South Florida, you met an old man who'd emerged from a forty-year-long coma into a world of weird new tech, children grown up overnight, and his own body withered as if by some curse—but when you asked him, "What's it like to Rip Van Winkle?" hoping for some insights, all he said was, "There's far less birds than I remember, far less birds flying around now, they're going away, we're losing them, they'll soon be gone."

WE THOUGHT WE LOST YOU...
WELCOME BACK

Look: it's 1924 in South Africa, where a scientist uses hammer, chisel, and knitting needle to separate limestone from a face, an infant's face complete with milk teeth, and while it's easy to imagine the scientist's pride as he names it *Australopithecus,* let us dream instead of what the child might say, if it could speak, after one million years of silence: *"So you see me, I didn't realize I wanted this but now I do, somebody sees me, and I'll go on being seen until the earth swallows me again."*

MY RESUME

I can weigh smoke, urinate in rainbow colors, unravel strands of my DNA and weave a smoking jacket from them; I can sweet-talk your hens into laying octagonal eggs and predict your daddy's fate (hint: he should have stayed in high school—and your mama didn't need that PhD); I can warm myself in a house on fire and get fresh air by cutting my throat; I can perfume my ears with *Hai Karate* and sleep beside a manta ray at the bottom of your swimming pool; when I'm angry, I can split rocks with my frown and when I'm thirsty, I can suck on clouds like popsicles; I can elevate your IQ using Silva Mind Control, plus I can moonwalk, even breakdance, to your favorite Elizabethan air—but I *can't* make you return my phone calls, and I'll feel stupid if I leave you one more voicemail.

DOJO LOGIC

The dreadlocked madman cleared out Pryna's local Starbucks in no time flat when he brandished a machete and hollered, "I'm gonna fucking cut your heads off!" but three days later Pryna found herself doing pushups beside the same guy at her white-belt karate class—how absurd that he was dressed in a *gi* like hers and gladly following their *sensei*'s orders!—so afterward, despite the danger, she asked this now surprisingly docile madman, "Didn't I see you this week at Starbucks?" and he gently stroked a dreadlock as he said, logically enough, "Which one?"

DOJO LOGIC: THE SEQUEL

Back at Pryna's Starbucks the following day, everybody scattered once more when the dreadlocked madman showed up with his machete, but Pryna stayed put, figuring, *We've met, so it'll look rude if I leave,* and she felt curious, besides, if he'd remember her—which he did, greeting Pryna with a hug and saying, "Hey, karate friend, I didn't catch your name last night, I'm Freddy, can I buy you a cup of coffee?"

PAVANE FOR A DEAD JEWISH PRINCESS

When Ethel was a girl, she loved to play "My Funny Valentine" on her piano, a Steinway Baby Grand, but Ethel's father, who had bigger plans for her, shook his head, saying, "Just play the classical, the serious stuff, those guys Ravel and Debussy and nothing but"—and after the marriage he'd arranged for her collapsed, leaving Ethel broken, she swore off playing music, every kind of music, and never touched that Steinway again until one night three decades later, the night before her death, when in a trance she left our kitchen in the middle of our meal, ignoring me, and found her way to her piano and started playing "My Funny Valentine," maybe hearing in that melody her fate, and while she played it all night long, no men were with her—no fathers, husbands, or even me, her only child— and at the time I thought that what she did was folly but now I think of it as grace, grace abounding to a girl who'd finally learned she needs nobody but herself.

CATCH OUR SOULS

First, the actor playing Iago heard his parents, who'd never been to a theater before, speaking loudly in the eighth row as they unwrapped and ate their dinner, prompting "Iago" to shout, "Be *quiet*, Mother!";

next, the actor who played Cassio, drunk because he'd caught his lover cheating, entered his big scene singing "Cabaret" and soon shifted to "The Surrey with the Fringe on Top";

and, finally, the actress playing Desdemona fell asleep after her death scene but soon awakened, still onstage, and sat up yawning, which caused the actor who played Othello to cuss her out and caused the audience to howl with laughter for the third time that star-crossed night.

WHO IS SHERRY DILLINGER AND WHAT IS SHE DOING IN AN ALLEY NEAR CHICAGO'S BIOGRAPH THEATER?

No one knew why twelve-year-old Sherry Kanopski of Chicago claimed to be the reincarnation of John Dillinger, infamous bank robber of the 1930s, but the girl took her claim far, insisting to everyone that her last name was actually his, studying all aspects of Dillinger's life, urging her parents to bring her to his birthplace, forcing her younger brother, Kenneth, to quiz her nightly on choice details of "Dillingeriana," as Sherry called it, and stealing her father's loaded handgun, then coaxing Kenneth to join her in the alley near the Biograph Theater where Melvin Purvis, G-man avenger, shot Dillinger down—a fact that Kenneth was well aware of as his sister placed the pistol in his hand and said, "Well, that Lady in Red tipped you off, I knew she would, and now your hunt is at an end—you *got* me, Purvis—so point the barrel at my chest and pull the trigger and when I'm lying on the ground, just use this dish towel I stole from Mom and dip it deep into the wound, saving my blood to sell on eBay for your reward."

THE DARKNESS AROUND US IS DEEP

As the tour guide informed you about the suffering of the inmates in this Auschwitz cellblock, you felt a light tap on your shoulder from a hand that wasn't there (and yet it *was*) and heard a harsh voice pass through lips that were not there (and yet they *were*), and this voice told you in Yiddish (which you don't speak, though somehow you could understand), "*He missed the bedbugs, he always does this, he forgot to mention bedbugs, but they were just as bad, believe me, as the lice.*"

WHO LOVES YA, BABY?

Each night in 1970 at Krishnamurti's school, where all electronic gadgets were banned, Meg heard faint voices and faint music seeping down from the bedroom above hers, Krishnamurti's own room, and after a week of sleeplessness she found the courage to mention those sounds to the old sage (whose joy, he said, came from his "never minding whatever happens") and after a moment of embarrassment he said to Meg, "Please don't repeat this to anyone, but every night I take a small gray Sony TV set from under my bed, and I watch *Kojak*...I must watch *Kojak*...I am *addicted*."

DEREK COMES ALIVE

"Since we've gotten to be so palsy-walsy on this ride," said the Cockney taxi driver as he drove Map through dense traffic to Map's hotel, "I might as well say how important today is, because it's the third anniversary of my suicide attempt, and even after a neighbor found me as I hung swinging from a pipe in my garage and cut me down—he was always coming over to borrow *tools*—my neck and throat were so damn bollocked that I spent weeks in hospital, three bloody weeks, just *agony*, and I kept cursing my fucking neighbor, but the day I started planning how I'd kill myself again, a school friend came around to visit, I hadn't seen the man in years, and he brought along his sister, eight years younger than us but she was *lovely*, and last Christmas in Majorca we got engaged, so let me say, mate, that if a day comes when you want to hang yourself, well, remember Der here at the wheel and think again," and as they drew close to Map's hotel, Map said, "When we get there, please park this

19

cab and climb right out, I want to hug you," and hug they did, these two near-strangers who held each other and ignored the hotel doorman who'd never seen a taxi journey end this way.

DEREK COMES ALIVE: THE SEQUEL

After Map recounted the Derek story to his old friend Jem's new wife, a Brazilian woman Map was meeting for the first time, she burst into tears and rushed to the restaurant bathroom, which confused Map until his friend said, "Laura's brother took his life last Easter," which made Map feel terrible, of course, but when she finally returned to their table, her cheeks still wet, Laura touched Map's arm and told him, "Don't say you're sorry, it's not your fault, you didn't know, and anyway your story's made me love my brother even more."

"IT'S ALL A JOKE"

Buried by an avalanche in the Rockies while driving alone in his Nissan, Tom made his peace with impending death by drinking from the beer keg he'd been bringing to his friend's house for a party, and when the need came, he managed to crack his window just enough to pee outside, which melted the snow packed like a wall there, melted it sufficiently for him to—*Eureka!*—claw at that snow with his fingers, and so that's how it went—*drink, piss, claw; drink, piss, claw*—until the rescue chopper found Tom, a drunk man staggering on hills of snow and laughing as he bellowed at the pilot, "*Not* one drop *left for you!*"

VOICI LES CLES: A TRIPLE PLAY

Once upon a time on the wall of a Miami Beach pizzeria there was a delicately painted mural in which gorgeous people in evening clothes sipped champagne, but two of these people, a pair of young men who stood together, had not been colored in—unlike the mural's other figures, they were merely outlined in black and white, like ghosts who'd crashed this many-hued party.

~~~

"That mural's artist was my friend," I told the pizzeria's new owner, "he was a charming Argentinean guy named Raul, and if you promise me you'll never get rid of the mural, I'll tell you all about it," to which the owner said, "I promise"—although he knocked down the mural's wall a few years later when he expanded his establishment.

~~~

"Raul was a waiter in this space in '92 when it was a café called 'Gertrude's,' and he was thrilled when Gertrude herself asked him to paint the mural, but he died soon after finishing it—and, yes, he *did* finish it, because he failed to color in those two 'ghosts' *on purpose*, he left them incomplete *on purpose*, those young men being Raul and his boyfriend, both killed by AIDS."

A CUSTODY BATTLE ACCOMPANIED
BY THE MUSIC OF BURT BACHARACH
AND HAL DAVID

Each time my parents fought over me, their only child—slapping, scratching, clawing, and kicking at each other while I stood watching, thumb in mouth—"Raindrops Keep Fallin' on My Head" and other lovely Bacharach/David songs would be playing on our turntable, or our car radio, or the jukebox in a diner, which makes me think that the music gods meant to console me, to stopper my ears with sweet sound, to give those ears something to focus on instead of "*What a fool I was to marry you*" and "*Boys need their fathers as much as their mothers*" and "*You'll get custody of him over my dead body, you bastard!*"

EDEN OR BUST

When I phoned the hospital room of my favorite college professor, who lay dying, an unfamiliar voice answered; and when I said, "Uh, hi, is Harold Poor there?" the voice said, "You must mean the previous patient, well, I'm sorry, he expired"; and once I worked out what "expired" meant, I remembered the last time I'd spoken with Poor, when he told me of a road trip his family made, driving into Florida during the Depression, and how the sudden appearance of trees hung with magical-seeming orange balls made Poor, a Bible-fed child, believe they'd found their way back to Eden.

I'M GOING TO HELL FOR THIS ONE

Because the business-suit-wearing Jesus freaks kept trying to convert her even after Pryna politely asked them to leave her be, she decided to have some fun, informing them that she "plays for the other team" ("*You mean you're a Satanist?*" "*Please, the correct term is* 'Luciferian'"); urging them to switch sides ("*Our parties are more fun than yours are, believe me*"); assuring them that Luciferians no longer sacrifice living beings ("*An animal rights wing in our coven put a stop to that*"); and warning them that her "team" would fare better come Armageddon ("*Our guy is gonna whip your guy, then nail him back on the cross where, this time, he'll stay put*").

THE NERVE OF LIFE TO CRASH OUR PARTY

What are we to make of the six-year-old girl who, when her father denied her a overpriced stuffed animal, complained to him, "But you don't get it—I *too* have a life," and what are we to make of her ten-year-old brother who consoled the girl by saying (loudly enough for Dad to hear), "I can't *wait* till we can put him in a nursing home"?

NAP ANYA, AHOY!

I love a woman who caresses trees and runs with fireflies and walks for miles on stormy nights, and who cares about insects as much as she does elephants, using Scotch Tape to repair torn spiderwebs, and who refers to her humble birdbath as a "health spa," and whose great wish is to live with creatures that need her help, and who met a deaf creature once, an Uber driver, and taught herself to sign during their ride so she could thank him in his language, and who misses her long-gone dog as if he left her only last week, and who would like to have her ashes scattered in every wild place she's known or else just have her body left out in one such place so that this place can gradually integrate her like the way she's come to love me.

SHORTIES: A PU PU PLATTER
WITH GUMBO SOUFFLE

When Gary's *döppelganger* finally caught up to him, Gary was losing at a game of go in an opium den called "Plotz," where the *döppelganger* said, "As you can see, I'm now a woman—call me 'Garita'—and I have a surgeon standing by who'll help you make the same change I made, which I insist on."

"No, I am *not* picking my nose," the child told her mother, "I'm massaging my brain, and these boogers I've been pasting on our sofa are *not* boogers—they're my bad memories."

I met a man on St. Mark's Place who was displaying his pet python, and when I asked him why it seemed so docile, he said, "Every morning we take a hot shower together."

〰〰〰

On their first date, Map boasted, "Osiris ate the sun, then shat me out," but Pryna, not impressed, replied, "Running out of water when she formed me, Isis mixed her tears into the clay."

〰〰〰

On a crowded street in Zurich I walked past Thuy Anh, whom I'd known at grad school in DC before her boyfriend murdered her, and once I turned and caught up to Thuy and said, "How can you *be* here, here in Zurich, when you're, like, *dead*?" she told me, "There's this secret relocation group—it's like the Witness Protection Program—for those of us who died young but aren't afraid to give our lives another go."

〰〰〰

Sometimes you feel like that funk guitarist who took so much LSD that his dead mother leaned out of her coffin to speak to him, and he answered her, and now he's living in the Pukersdorf asylum where their conversation goes on and on.

〰〰〰

Standing by his side, I cheered on my son as he played pinball, and sure enough, he went on winning, racking up an impressive score, and so the seasons passed, as did the years, and then the years turned into decades and both of us grew old together at that machine, in the arcade that was now, apart from us, empty and still.

〰〰〰

"No, dear," Pryna told me, "by 'give you head,' I meant I'd lick, and suck, and nibble on *your mind*."

"Good luck," I said after giving some coins to a grinning homeless man who sat atop a tower of garbage, but my words made him stop grinning and "*Hey*," he called after me, "I don't need you to wish me *that*, man—I *am* lucky."

Of the thousand sons of Somnus, god of sleep, only Morpheus, who engineers our dreams, can appear to us in human form, so he must have been that plump guy with the goatee who elbowed you in your most recent nightmare and said, "All the strangers you see in dreams except for me are other dreamers."

What if Alexander the Great got separated from his army during a battle and found himself alone in some grove where it dawned on him that every tree here had a unique yet finite existence and where, once he realized that this truth applied as well to all his soldiers, he sat on a fallen poplar's trunk and wept?

"And where are *you* from, young man?" the esteemed Judge Waltz's widow asked a first-year Yale Law student at a banquet, and when he answered, "Ohio," she looked embarrassed for him and leaned forward to whisper, "*Please*, here in New Haven we pronounce it *Iowa*."

"I guess that wasn't exactly a happy landing," said my father in 1940 when he washed out of pilot training by crashing his plane during his first flight, but the instructor seated beside him gave him one last lesson by saying, in a thick Alabaman accent, "Bud, any landing you walk away from is a happy landing."

Ashamed about being drunk at his cousin's funeral—so drunk that he had to ask his taxi driver to help him knot his necktie—Map advised himself before arriving, *Just say "I'm sorry," to all the mourners and you'll be fine*, though the first person he said "I'm sorry" to replied, "Thank you, sir, but I'm the fellow who drove the hearse."

A veteran bar-fighter, Harry was—and yet he still surprised me when he phoned me from the ER saying, "I got in a goddamn knife fight," to which I said, "But you've been wheelchair-bound for years, who'd stab an old coot like you in that condition?" and Harry answered, "That punk was in a wheelchair, too."

"Yeah, we see some weirdness," said the cellphone repairperson, "like the guy whose ex-girlfriend keeps texting him no matter how much he changes his number—she always gets his new digits somehow—and what she writes is, 'I miss you here, please come and join me,' which is creepy because this ex died in a car crash three years back."

People always said my mother looked like Eva Braun, so as soon as I was old enough to know what's what, I grew the moustache to match her.

Still speaking little English after three weeks spent in Tampa, the Brazilian hippie Cesar decided to see New York, so he caught a ride on the interstate from a very friendly trucker, and two days later that trucker left Cesar at an IHOP, telling him, "You're in Times Square, man," but a waitress there gave Cesar free coffee before she broke the news to him: he was in Texas.

✎✎✎

"Help," said the woman who took Borges's hand while he stood at the traffic crossing, and because he was blind and unfamiliar with this place, he accepted her assistance, and after they'd crossed the street, these strangers parted ways, with Borges never knowing that the woman had been as blind as he was and that her offer of "help" was actually a request.

✎✎✎

From childhood on, my Danish friend Jens suffered from nightmares in which a small word appeared before his eyes, a word he sensed would someday spell his doom, but he failed to understand what this word meant until he visited New Orleans and a large truck with the word "MACK" on its front grille bore down on him.

✎✎✎

Imprisoned in Prague for refusing to be a soldier, Jurgen was surprised during a few months in the eighties when he and his fellow inmates got fresh salad, heaps of salad (until that time, all they'd gotten was bread and foul wurst)—but decades later, in his new, post-Communist home, he read the paper one fine day and learned the reason for the salad: all those vegetables had been harvested from the farms around Chernobyl.

On our third date I took V. to a shooting range, assuming she'd never used a handgun before, but after I playfully arranged my sweater over the target, she shot a perfect ring of bullet holes around the sweater's heart and then said, faintly smiling, "Just so you know."

✺

"Stay in school," the old Jewish man walking his dog told the timid Cuban boy, "steer clear of gangs, read lots of books, find a good job, keep your nose clean"—and only after this man died did the boy learn that "*Tio* Meyer," as all his neighbors in Miami Beach called him, had a last name, which was "Lansky."

✺

"Sorry, sir, but I need you to bend over," the moon-faced TSA agent told me after I'd gone through the airport security checkpoint, and on seeing my surprised look (*Bend over? Right here? In front of* everyone?), the agent laughed and pointed to my laptop, on which I'd recently pasted (but forgotten) a bumper-sticker reading, "SPANK ME."

✺

Marsha was losing her vision, *fast*, and she made sure that everybody at her workplace felt guilty about it—why should it be *her* instead of *them*?—until the day when, out of the usual polite murmurs of regret, rose the voice of a colleague who said, "I really wish you weren't going blind, Marsh, but I will *not* give you my eyes."

✺

Inspired by the German aphorist Lichtenberg's quip that "Anyone can sleep with the Queen of England if their desire for it is great enough and they devote themselves to nothing else," Luther Bix developed a plan and followed it, step-by-step, until that aged English monarch lay naked before him, but then Bix—well, to quote Lichtenberg again, "Never before had a mind come to such a majestic halt."

~

"Does your kid like *Star Wars*?" the crusty old taxi driver asked, and when my son, who'd just turned six, spoke up before I did, saying, "Oh, *yeah*," the cabbie announced, with obvious pride, "Well, sonny, that English actor who plays Obi-Wan Kenobi gave some young guy a blow job *right* where you're sitting!"

~

When you said, "How goes it?" to the bearded man who stood beside you at the Bob Neuwirth concert, just making polite conversation, he pondered for awhile before he said, "Well, I'm *upright*, and I'm *coherent*, so that makes two out of three, I guess," and when you asked him, "What's the third thing?" he pondered this new question for even longer before he told you, "No one knows."

FROM KETHER TO MALKUTH

The race car champion's advice about regular driving—"*Always pay attention*"—casts your mind back to your first memory, that morning before dawn when you awakened on your own (no happy mother to sing you "Rise and Shine"; she was still sleeping) and up you stood there in your crib, each pink fist gripping a wooden slat as you peered into the dark beyond your window until—*shazam!*—the sky (as if some switch got thrown) filled instantly with light, a sudden impossible sunrise that seemed to say, "*Now that I've gotten your attention...*"

THE HAWK MUST SWOOP

At the Metropolitan Club, a hired assassin told you facts about himself—that he had zero fear of death; that, on retirement, he planned to murder his private enemies on his own dime; and that he'd once convinced a rival hit man not to kill him simply through logical persuasion—but what you found most charming, *and* most believable, was that a toothache once drove this assassin half-mad, because, he said, "I'm not afraid of death, no, but pain can drive me round the frigging *bend*."

RUN, VERNITA, RUN

I met Vernita Wheat in a Carson City thrift shop, where we got to chatting, and she claimed to be "the sole surviving member of Pawnee Bill's Wild West Show" ("Pawnee Bill was Buffalo Bill's biggest competitor," she explained), and before I could ask her what work she'd done there, Vernita tapped her soiled yellow ski cap with a bony finger, dipped that finger in a pocket, drew from it a sheet of paper, gave this wrinkled sheet to me, and said, "Read it and weep, son," which I did, thereby learning all about her from this brief memoir she'd scrawled in pencil, a memoir beginning with "*1895, Born to Theodore and Laura Wheat (née Tyler) at 1439 Dumaine Street, New Orleans,*" and telling of a troubled childhood and several marriages and several children as well as travel to two "different continents," and ending with "*1981, Escaped from The President And First Lady Nursing Home Of Sioux Falls, South Dakota, and resumed life on the road,*" and as I handed the paper back to her, I said, "Can I buy you a cup of coffee?" to which she grinned a gummy grin and said, "Gosh, I'd rather you bought me *boots*, son," and then, pointing to a used pair of snakeskins (some scales were peeling off, but those boots still looked sharp), "*there,*" Vernita said, "that pair will do."

THE RIVER GIRL

Every afternoon the family of female elephants were led by their young *mahout* along the same road through the jungle to the muddy river where they bathed—and today, while standing on the riverbank, you watched as one of the "older girls," as the *mahout* calls them, went romping through the water like the world's most jubilant child, slashing the surface with her trunk, rolling over on her back, sinking slowly, going, going, until reemerging into air—*surprise!*—and she refuses to end her playtime despite the *mahout*'s urgent shout, pure temporary life having so much fun that it might as well be eternal.

LICKING HONEY FROM A THORN

With certain paintings, my favorite parts are the details you'll miss if you don't look closely enough—I gasped in one museum, for instance, when I caught sight of Dante in the picture *Marriage of Beatrice*, Dante just another face in a festive crowd, but a face racked with misery because his muse has just married another man—and then, a few years later, I gasped again in a different museum when I looked at a Gallen-Kallela canvas in which a young woman (it could have been the newlywed Beatrice) watches some workmen build a house for her family but one of the workmen's faces, she's failed to notice (not looking closely enough), is made of bone, a grinning skull, Death stealing into her happiness—as was the case with Beatrice, who, to Dante's further misery, died young.

CREATURE FEATURE

The man in the Indianapolis bar said, "People warned us the house was haunted, but I didn't believe in ghosts, not even after the freakish odors and the mysteriously slamming doors and the shadow-shapes our daughter glimpsed, but then I had a nightmare where I was looking in our freezer and stacked inside it were severed heads, and I was screaming when our phone rang, waking me up, and it kept ringing till my wife grabbed it and said, 'Hello?...What? *What*?' and then she told me, '*That* was odd—some hoarse guy whispered, 'Ask your husband how he likes the gifts I left you in my old freezer.'"

UNDER ENCHANTMENT

34 Four teenage boys, all tripping on mescaline, walked into a men's room in Disneyland in 1990, but only three of them came out—the fourth stepped by accident through a door labeled "*Staff Only*" and wound up wandering through the tunnels meant for Magic Kingdom workers, those costumed characters who use the tunnels to rush from one point to another, and that lost boy is down there still, his mind continually blown by each generation of silly creatures who mock his plight and who refuse to help him leave.

MILLBURN

Tonight you're thinking of a child who saw a pigeon outside his window and reached to touch it, and how the pigeon flew away but the child couldn't fly, and how he fell and fell and fell and then stopped falling, and how his father expressed his grief by bashing his head against a wall, and how his mother destroyed the child's photos because to see them hurt too much, and how in time they dared to have another child (they hadn't planned to before their loss) and how this child then had a child of her own, and so you're thinking of the uncle you never met and of the likelihood you owe your life to his failed attempt to touch a pigeon.

BE GROOVY OR LEAVE

When the teacher who leads their meditation class called in sick today, her replacement was a woman with feathered-back hair who announced, "My name is Phoenix, and I'm joined today by my spiritual comrade Rafael, who right this moment is perched on the shoulder of that man in the fuchsia T-shirt who's scowling at me as if he doesn't believe a word I say," and as Map looked at his right shoulder, just to confirm no "spiritual comrade" was perched there, Phoenix said, "Oh, *no*, mister, don't bother—Raffy won't let himself be seen by any rude scowlers like *you*."

"I'M HERE TO HELP," SAYS LORNA LIEBMILCH

Of all the weapons in superheroine Lorna Liebmilch's crime-fighting arsenal—

filed-down false teeth; suction cups; mini-bazookas and toxic breath strips; a cat-o'-nine-tails; 5D goggles; an outlawed cough syrup called "Mucaquell"; *shurikens* and *nunchakus* and other ninja gear; ready-mix artificial lava; a Boy Scout uniform (*"It came in handy when I was tracking these mutant fur trappers in Yosemite,"* says Lorna); pain-relieving chewing gum; disfiguring lip gloss; gris-gris bags and working mojos (last used in combat against the Haitian zombie Bredda Gravalicious); a mini-PA system that blares REO Speedwagon music (meant to demoralize the enemy); saltpeter capsules (*"They came in handy when I took down that sex-mad pro wrestler Onan the Librarian"*); methane explosives, dart-blowers, mousetraps, and Shlabotnik thrusting spears; the Indian sex manual *Pokam*, with its famed "peacock embrace" (*"The best tome of its kind I've ever come upon"*); elixirs causing the temporary onset of "foul foot" and "scurfy ear"; a lightweight Gatling gun (*"It came in handy when I was fighting these Civil War reenactors run amok"*); anti-brainwashing Jello; a combination vibrator/power drill (*"Don't forget which button is which!"*); quinine Band-Aids and fast-acting anti-venom spray for jungle work; plus a First-Aid kit and a change of dry socks—

of all these weapons, few are more effective than Lorna's ability to regard *nothing*, not even death, "with *too* much seriousness," since, as she explains, "Angels fly because they take themselves lightly."

SWEET AS APPLE CIDER

My great-aunt Ida was a flapper and then got married and had a daughter, an only child, who caught the flu but then in a hospital caught meningitis, which brought on brain damage and left her living in a clinic where Ida visited till her girl died, and then came Ida's own turn to die, and in the hospice I held her hand as her breathing slowed, slowed, slowed, and finally stopped—I'd never witnessed a death before—and when I gathered Ida's things, I found a photo of her daughter, the girl before the meningitis, and even though I never met her, I now display this photo in my home so that someone, at least *one* person, will still remember Ida's child, whose name was Ellen.

FREAK-OUTS, SHAKE-UPS, AND LETDOWNS

Looking back after it ended, Pryna Pamlig realized that her love affair with Map Grylapin had felt emotionally much like a scene from the TV show *The Prisoner*, a scene in which the hero starts to drink a pint of Guinness, finds the word "YOU" engraved on the glass's bottom, then drinks some more and sees the word "JUST," then drinks some more and sees the word "DRANK," and finally, draining the glass, he sees the last word, which is "POISON."

SHOUT OUT OVER THE WATER: "I WON'T BE HERE LONG"

In the graveyard of a remote Norwegian village is a most unusual marker: not a stone but a rusted pink propeller from the airplane of a German fighter pilot who'd crashed nearby at the war's end and whose parents would journey from Munich to that village every June until one year when they stopped coming, leaving that propeller grave unnoticed except by local children who'll stare at it sometimes, trying to guess what the object means before they grow up and turn their thoughts to more important things.

SCROOGE SCHOOL

"Old Mean Mac," we called our third grade teacher, because Mrs. McIntyre was a sadist, a real old-fashioned battle-axe dealing out harsh discipline to one and all, and we assumed when her son died in a car wreck that she would now treat us worse than ever, but when she came back a week after his funeral, she was different, completely different, merely smiling a spooky smile at us and saying nothing as we began to break her rules, and by the afternoon, chaos reigned, and we spilled out to the hallway, pretending to be pirates, using rulers as our swords, and soon the headmaster showed up and yelled, "Mrs. McIntyre, *do something*!" but she just turned her spooky smile to him and said, "Take a good look at these children—they move, they talk, they laugh, they *breathe*—how can we improve them?," and, without waiting for an answer, she got up and left our classroom, "Old Mean Mac" no longer, and found some pirates and watched their sword fight.

PALE RED

"This is *not* a birthmark on my forehead," said the stranger with blue suede shoes seated beside me on the 6 train, "no, this is a symbol I placed here myself because eons ago I was a monarch, I ruled this world, and one day my vizier came to me announcing that all my subjects soon would go insane, every person barking mad, yet with his magic he'd be able to rescue us, just me and him, we'd be the only living sane ones, yet just in case we got split up, we put this symbol on our foreheads, a pale red marking so we could recognize each other, and over time I *did* lose him, or *he* lost *me*, I can't recall, and ever since then I've been searching for my vizier, trying to spot our symbol on the foreheads of you strangers, you poor mad people, but all I find are frown-lines, and ash-dabs, and birthmarks that *look like* our symbol…but no, not really."

TABASCO SAUCE, WEAPONIZED

"Hide this Tabasco sauce bottle in your pocket," the divorcée told her child, "and tonight at Fong's Garden when they serve that bastard his pork lo mein, pull out the bottle, twist the top off, pour the hot sauce all over his food, and then shout so the whole restaurant can hear, 'This is what you get for abandoning me and my mother, you homewrecker, you!'"

THINKING OF RICHARD BRAUTIGAN
AND OTHER NICE THINGS

Every morning for six years while walking through San Francisco's Washington Square, Map would say "Hi" to the statue of Benjamin Franklin, the one whose pedestal reads, "PRESENTED BY H. D. COGSWELL TO OUR BOYS AND GIRLS WHO WILL SOON TAKE OUR PLACES AND PASS ON," but Ben Franklin never replied to Map until the day when he said, "Say, young man, you've got a bit of omelet on your moustache," and when Map asked, while wiping the egg off, "How come you're only speaking *now*?," Ben replied, "Before today your moustache was always clean."

IN WHICH THE READER IS INVITED TO
DISCOVER A CERTAIN GAME

It was a banal late-nineties Brooklyn love affair, but you think of Maxine often—not of *her*, exactly, but of her brother, the teenage brother she often spoke about, the brother who for months lay in a coma but then one afternoon woke up (soon he'd be comatose again, and would die the following week), woke up that day in his hospital room, looked at his parents and his sister, then said to them, as if delivering great news, eyes opened wide, filled with amazement, "It's just *a game*, guys, nothing else, it's just *a game*, so play that *game*, guys, that's all you need to do, just *play* it, *play* it..."

THEY CALL HER "CANDY THUNDER"

Map hadn't realized how drunk the blond young woman was—
they'd only just met in a bar—until she invited him to her condo
and they climbed into her Mustang and she promptly cut off two
lanes of Sunset traffic, which made Map holler, *"Pull over, let me
out,"* but the woman just laughed at this and punched Map in the
mouth, then turned her fist into a claw and seized his own hand
and jammed it under her whoops-no-undies sundress, yelling—
as she sideswiped a parked car—"Amuse me till we get there."

WANDERING STAR

At last week's conference, the first astronomer said, "We'd like
to know more about the supernova our ancestors witnessed in
1054 CE," and the second astronomer said, "We'd like to know
more about Jupiter's moon Europa, whose sub-ice ocean may
well harbor myriad life-forms," and then the third astronomer
said, "I want to know why our son Tim ran off when he was
fifteen, and where he is now, and if he's safe, and if he knows
how much I miss him, and if I'll ever see him again."

LIFE IS A DRUG THAT STOPS WORKING

We all dropped LSD at a friend's house in the Hamptons, but growing weary of socializing, I decided to take a walk beneath a swollen-looking moon, and soon I came upon a cemetery that I wandered through, looking at the gravestones lit by moonlight, and all of a sudden I heard these *voices* come issuing from this one moss-covered grave—a rising chorus of moaning voices—and though I told myself, *It's just the acid, just an auditory hallucination, it* can't be *ghosts*, I shouted, "Oh, *shit*," anyway, and swung around and ran back to my friend's house, and when I told my story there, everybody seemed impressed except for one woman who said, "Dude, it *was* ghosts, and you intruded in their home, you weren't invited, so you should go back and apologize," which in my drugged state made good sense (I didn't believe in spirits, yet didn't want to be cursed by any, either),

and so I forced myself to walk to that graveyard again, with the swollen-looking moon not making me feel any less scared, and I almost gave up three times but finally got to the outer gate, where I heard a burst of rustling movement and glimpsed a burst of silver movement—that cemetery had come alive with frantic movement!—but just before I turned to run like hell, I could see the movement's source, which were *deer*, a dozen deer who had gathered in that place, making it theirs, and as I caught my breath, shock wearing off, I told myself how sweet it is that our graveyards fill up at night with life.

HISTORY'S DEFUNCT PROFESSIONS: #4382

It was long past midnight, Broadway's sidewalks were almost empty, and the squirrely man with greasy long hair rooted around with a thin curved gray wire inside the payphone next to the one Pryna used—back in the eighties, these phones were often set beside each other in the open air—and when she finished her call, Pryna asked the man what he was doing, a question he answered without glancing up from his labors: "Robbing the coins, of course, I make two hundred bucks a night, but I suggest you move along, doll, because this new kind of phone is giving me trouble, they built it to be theft-proof, and you're distracting me."

LET'S GO THUNDERING

"Keep on thundering," she used to say, she who was rock 'n' roll made flesh, she who was born just as Neil Armstrong took his moon walk, she who would soar in childhood dreams above her hometown, smelling gas from a local refinery, and now that she's dead, I want to soar, too, across the ocean and back through time into a Stockholm summer evening in the nineties, when we're still young and she's still healthy, and in a nightclub there she's raised her hand for me, extending it with a cute flourish, and she will go on doing this until it's my own turn to die, a moment I'll probably mar with my complaining—I do still struggle to "let go," though letting go, she tried to teach me, that's where the thunder and the moon and rock 'n' roll are coming from—and yet this moment when we first meet, this let-go moment, this moment *now*, I'm leaning forward to kiss her hand, and as I do—

"Call me Mad Madeleine," she says.

GOOFY

First my Norwegian ex-girlfriend frowned at her first taste of an orange cake in a Paris restaurant, saying, "Why does this dessert taste like salmon?" (evidently the cook had not washed her plate well enough after its previous course of fish) and *then*, a decade later, my Hungarian wife in a restaurant in New York took a bite of her entrée whose sauce was overly sweet and said with a frown, "Why does this salmon taste like dessert?," so I smiled and thought, *Different women, different cities, different times, but the same thing in reverse—not only do the gods exist, but they have a goofy sense of humor.*

AN ASS-PINCHER IN ISTANBUL

44   Furious at the guy who'd just pinched his girlfriend's ass, Map stalked after the ass-pincher and blocked his way on the sidewalk, shouting, "*Eyup*, motherfucker, *eyup*," which he'd learned from his guidebook is the Turkish word for "shame on you," but the ass-pincher didn't seem to understand, much less look chastened—in fact, he even strangely used his finger to point somewhere—and later on Map told this story to a Turkish friend who laughed, saying, "No, no, you mispronounced the word, we say 'shame on you' as '*ay-yip*,' not as '*ay-yup*,'" so Map said, "Then what did I tell that ass-pincher?" and his friend laughed some more and said, "It's the name of a district here in Istanbul—he thought you rudely asked him for directions."

NOSE DEEP

It was an allergy attack that woke you up in your tent on the shores of Lake Manyara, but it was the growling of a lion right outside the tent that kept you awake, awake and frightened, and once you realized it was your sneezing that was making the lion growl, agitating it more and more, you tried hard not to sneeze but found you couldn't, because the one thing you're allergic to is cats, and now you and this big cat made for a most dysfunctional couple.

MEMORIES OF COLONEL SANDERS

As I looked with pleasure at the painting called *Colonel Sanders Fries In Hell*, I told the gallery's owner, "Believe it or not, when I was five back in 1968, I met the Colonel in the lobby of the Fontainebleau Hotel, though as I grew up, I began to doubt this memory—I mean, had I just imagined it?—but then last year in London I visited my friend Bart, who had a photo of a teenage boy shaking hands with Colonel Sanders, and when I asked him about it, Bart said, 'That's me meeting the KFC guy at the Fontainebleau in '68.'"

WOULD YOU HIRE THIS PERSON?

Pryna had fun at her job interview with Bix Corp, answering the question "*Do you believe in God?*" with "I believe in *all* gods, just for kicks"; "*describing*" herself "*in five words*" as "lucky, lucky, lucky (and) very grateful"; saying, "Both my sets of grandparents, maternal and paternal, are named David and Lena" when asked to "*tell us something unique about yourself*"; and announcing that her "*favorite joke*" is, "When a traveling salesman comes to a house and rings the bell and the front door is opened by a ten-year-old boy who's wearing his mother's brassiere, the salesman is shocked but still manages to say, 'Are your parents home?' to which the boy replies, 'What do *you* think?'"

WOULD YOU HIRE THIS PERSON?: THE SEQUEL

First, the Bix Corp interviewer, a beautiful Hungarian lawyer, smiled at Pryna's "favorite joke," then she said (right before she told Pryna, "You're hired"), "A better punch line might be if the boy wearing the bra, when he's asked if his parents are home, says, 'Who do you think are making me wear this?'"

CURTAINS

"Oh, you're that guy who shook hands with John Kennedy," I'd always say when I encountered Jules, a homeless man whose long gray hair hung like curtains that hid his face (he'd told me, the first time we shared a park bench, how his father once took him to a rally for JFK), and I also remember Jules saying, "The worst thing about being homeless is how you've got no privacy," which might explain, come to think of it, those curtains.

IMPROVED BY VERKA

Once the old man got the news that made his heart soar, he started speaking to the groundhogs in the park where he walked daily, trying to communicate with these creatures, but they said nothing, they simply scurried down their holes when he approached, and after two weeks he decided to cram his body into one hole, which was empty—though it was dark there, so maybe not—and as he breathed in the scent of soil, he said, "I mean you no harm, fellas, I just want to share some great news that I got."

APPROVED BY GABOU

As for the robin who flew into our kitchen window, wrongly believing that the sky she saw reflected in the glass unscrolled forever, we buried her broken body, pretending that she'd appeared before or after our home's existence, meaning the sky *would* keep unscrolling and she could fly without growing weary in a race with time itself, a race she'd win at last when God, the referee, would say, "Robin, you impress me, and for your prize, please take my place here in my nest, since unlike you, I *have* grown weary, so weary death will be my friend."

HERE AT THE SHRINER FAIR

To the Shriner Fair my father brought me—to "*The Essex County Shriners' Fun-Fair For Legally Separated Or Divorced Men And Their Children*"—but he said no when I asked to try out the fearsome ride called "King Whirl"—" It looks too wild," he said, "and, anyway, you just ate"—but I manipulated him, as usual, saying, "*Mom* would let me do it," so finally he gave in—"But I'm going on that thing *with* you"—and King Whirl spun us around and shook us up so much that when we finally stumbled off it, the two of us felt sick, our stomachs rumbling, and yet I never felt so close to him, or would again, as I felt right when we both began to puke, his arm around me, father and son brought low together, our vomit mixing in the sawdust.

THIS BABALAWO'S FOR HIRE

When their relationship was crumbling, Pryna and Map sought advice from a *babalawo*, but this priest of the Nigerian religion of *Ifá* turned out to be a middle-aged Jewish guy who'd been a big wheel in real estate, whose desk in his Malibu beach house was cluttered with stones and bones and seashells, who advised Pryna and Map to throw ripe fruit into the ocean to save their love (spoiler alert: that didn't help), who kept whispering to his newborn girl, "*Eshu* loves you, *Eshu* loves you," and who—speaking of children—told the couple that they would have their own child together (spoiler alert: they never did) and that this child would grow up to be a *babalawo*, too.

THREE VERSIONS OF AHASUERUS

The old man in the homeless shelter claimed to be Ahasuerus, the Wandering Jew, that legendary immortal who'd been condemned to walk the earth because of his casual cruelty to Jesus, but after he disappeared, someone suggested that he was actually just some wretch who'd been driven mad by guilt for rejecting his junkie daughter, a young woman who because of that rejection died;

then someone else shook her head, saying, "No, you just stole that explanation from a story in the O. Henry book we've been passing around here"—

so now we don't know what to think.

LOLLIPOPS FOR EVERYONE

"The only passenger I ever picked up twice," said your loquacious taxi driver as he drove you across the Triborough Bridge, "was this businessman who gave me trouble on both rides—first, he had his girlfriend along, *smoochy smoochy*, we dropped her off at her rowhouse in Queens, and when we got to *his own* digs, this big McMansion on Long Island, his wife came running across their lawn to question me if he'd been riding with any chippies, which I knew to lie about, and sure enough, he gave me a crazy-big tip for that, but the second time I drove him—I recognized him right away—he was alone and stinking drunk, and when I pulled up to his house, he was out cold, just stone unconscious, and no matter how much I shook him, he wouldn't wake up, so I dragged him from my back seat to his lawn—no wife this time, I rang the doorbell, she didn't answer—and then I pulled his wallet out to get my fare (plus, *sure*, a good tip for my trouble, why not) but all he had was thirteen bucks, not enough, so in the end I yanked his shoes off and took his socks, which were *nice*, man, silk or something, matter of fact—" (and here your cabbie turned to grin at you while nearly ramming into a Buick)—"I'm wearing those socks right now."

THIS DREAM IS SHORT BUT
THIS DREAM IS HAPPY

As the young nurse fed teaspoons of watery oatmeal to the old man, the old man's mother hovered nearby, a watchful ghost who felt so grateful to the nurse that at one point she said (though she knew the nurse couldn't hear her), "Thanks for taking care of my little boy."

HAVE YE NO DREDE (STORY VIA AL)

Having lost her self-confidence tonight, the actor refused to go onstage in this local production of *The Crucible*, but onstage she finally did go (her costars had pressured her into it), and ten minutes through the first act she noticed a pair of bright eyes in the audience—she couldn't see the face they belonged to, or see *any* faces, but she could make out the audience's eyes—and *these* specific eyes, they watched her work from the third row's aisle seat with such *attention*, such *approval*, that she thought, *Whoever you are, you're my* savior, *you're making all of this feel worth it, beaming hope in my direction,* and she played all night to those eyes, to that savior, but when the houselights came up at last and the actors walked back onstage to take their bows, she saw that those eyes belonged to someone's seeing-eye dog.

AND NOW, A VALUABLE TIP FOR
THE NEWLY DEAD...

As Charon ferried me across the River Styx, I finally accepted that I'd bought the farm, but because I didn't want to bring along this one bad memory (you know what you did, Mary M.), I dipped my hand in the oily water, cupped some into my mouth and gulped it down, hoping it might confer amnesia the way the River Lethe is said to, and Charon yelled, "That's not allowed!" but he was too late because—*shazam!*—my naughty sipping from the Styx whooshed me out of that boat and back to life, back to *my* life, right at the moment when I'd lost it, giving me a second chance, the chance to put down the syringe, and now I'm laughing my lucky ass off at that Charon, and at the gods, and at *you*, Mary—laughing straight into a new day.

ROCK 'N' ROLL HERNIA (1)

"Why are you wearing greasepaint on your face?" the talk-show host asks the Kabbalah-savvy rock star Benny Pompa, who, seeming surprised by the question, touches his left cheek with a fingertip, licks the greasepaint off of it, considers the taste for a moment, then says, "What face?"

WOLF SETS THE SCENE

Instead of giving me advice when I got into a fix, my uncle Wolf would tell me this story: "*Once there was a man who took a wrong step while picking berries and tumbled over a steep cliff, and though he was able to grab a tree branch as he fell, that branch began to weaken—and once it snapped, he knew, his fall would kill him—so the man prayed to God for guidance, hollering, 'What can I do, God, what can I do?' and God did answer, in a voice that really boomed, with only two words, namely: 'Let go.'*"

COME, JOSEPHINE,
IN MY SWINGING MACHINE

In Chicago there's a nightclub that's called "Swing Squared" because in the front room, couples do "the Bijou" and "the Prancer" and other forms of "swing dance" while in the back room later on these couples remove their clothes and practice a different form of "swinging" (which is why a sign there reads, "PLEASE COVER YOUR LOWER TORSO AT THE FOOD BAR"), and the bartender at this club calls himself "Empress Josephine" because he believes that he's the reincarnation of Napoleon's first wife (although the closest he ever really got to the Little Corporal was at Waterloo, where in his one past life this bartender was a Prussian officer's horse).

SPARKS FLY UPWARD

This salvia is supposed to get you high super-fast, but it's not working, it's a dud, Pryna told herself as she placed the metal pipe and plastic lighter on her bed at the Amsterdam Hilton (the same hotel where the Dutch rock star Herman Brood once leaped from the roof), and she was wondering about a refund when the left side of her body floated to the ceiling while her right side remained in place, and soon she was watching a lovely flame that sprang up beside her until the salvia wore off and Pryna found out that the lighter she'd set down on the bedspead had set her bed on fire.

WHAT THE DWARF KING SAID

54   From his throne atop the bar, the dwarf king watched us dancing in *Nave Jungla,* or "Jungle Spaceship"—the Buenos Aires nightclub where the staff, from bartenders to bouncers, were little people, and where the dance floor was packed with bikers, and where the music was Electric Light Orchestra, and where the song "Mr. Blue Sky" stopped abruptly, and then in the silence that followed we all turned to face the king, who stood unsteadily, adjusted his crown, opened a leather-bound book he'd been clutching in his lap, blew dust from its first page (or pretended to), and read silently for a moment (only slightly moving his lips) before he told us in a child's voice, "To be...or NOT be...IT'S A QUESTION!"

K-K-K-K-K-K-K-K

When Pryna did a good deed, buying a cup of coffee for a stranger with some terrible neurological condition, he sat up in his chair at the café and pointed to the cup she gave him and looked at her and said, "K-k-k-k-k-k..."

("Yes?" she replied, assuming he meant to say "coffee"...)

"-k-k-k-k-k-k-k..."

(and Pryna smiled reassuringly, as if to say, "Don't worry, I'll be patient until you get the word out"...)

"-k-k-k-k-k-k-k-k..."

("*Coffee,*" right, I get it, I guess I'll be here for a while...)

And she did keep waiting, waiting and smiling, till he could finally finish his word, which was "k-k-k-k-k-k-k-k-k-k-k-KIND."

STRAWBERRY (1) (VIVA BARBARA P.)

Map's second favorite moment today was when he watched an old woman in a sundress run past him in the Luxembourg Gardens—running awkwardly, as you'd expect of someone her age, but with the eagerness of a child—and Map's very favorite moment today was when that woman came walking back, no longer in a hurry, and this time she held and licked a strawberry ice cream cone.

HOLD YOUR MUD: A TRIPLE PLAY

"Sorry you got three Fs on your report card," I told my friend's freckled tenth-grader, but she just shrugged and said, "As long as I'm not in prison or the hospital, I'm good as gold."

~~~~~

"Sorry you're under armed guard in a prison hospital," I told this girl a few months later, but she just shrugged, still unfazed, and said, "Even if I go to hell, I'll find a way to enjoy it."

~~~~~

"Sorry you've been condemned to a lake of fire in the eighth circle of hell," I told this girl a few months later, but she just shrugged, plainly unsinkable, and said, "As long as I'm alive and smart, I can figure out the rest."

THE TORTURE RARELY STOPS

The third time Map paid (top-dollar) for an hour-long session at a discreet dungeon uptown, the mistress had just started to work him over with her new iron paddle when she sneezed, then sneezed again, and soon it got so bad that she had to raise her mask and wipe her nose with her leather-covered forearm—"It's just hay fever," she explained, her blue eyes watery—and even though she tried to keep their session going, in the end she had to call it off, remove that mask, blow her nose with a wad of Kleenex, and say to Map, "Jeez, sorry, honey, bad allergy day, you'll get a refund."

A BAR MITZVAH WITH MUSCLE

All happy Bar Mitzvahs are alike, but each unhappy Bar Mitzvah is unhappy in its own way, with Map's own festivities going bad when his estranged father stormed into the ballroom shouting, "I have every right to be here!" and the thugs hired by Map's mother—"muscle from Newark," she'd called them, having guessed that *he* would show up—got busy pummeling the trespasser while everyone, except for Map, cheered on that muscle.

SO THIS IS THE FOREST OF ARDEN!

"Don't worry," I tell the buck that has just one antler, "you'll grow a new pair come springtime, that's how this deal goes, but eventually you'll vanish and I'll remember meeting you when I keep walking through this forest until it's my own turn to vanish, after which a different boy and different buck will maybe meet here, unaware that *we* existed, but it's okay, that too comes with this deal"—although by now the buck has turned and run from me, strong winter light on that single antler.

WHAT THE OLD ONES HAVE IN MIND

When our starship landed on Saturn and we began to set up our first colony, we were surprised to find that two ancients, Li Po and Tu Fu, had preceded us there, and now they stood together on a bridge composing poems about autumn leaves, then tossing these poems into the phosphorescent river.

OLFACTORY SORROW

"Your daughter cries a lot when she's in class," the third-grade teacher emailed to the widower, who was unhappily surprised by this—hadn't his girl turned the corner back in March?—but then he met the teacher for the first time and smelled on her the same perfume his dead wife wore.

STEVE THE DRUID SURFER REPEALING THE LAWS OF TIME

After two years of rambling around, my sister and I made a home for ourselves in Zuma Beach, and every week we'd hike to a cove where no one else ever seemed to go until the day when we came upon five gangbangers picnicking there *and* a dozen bikini models who lounged around for a photoshoot *and* this sinewy nude dreadlocked man who wore a tribal mask and kept on dancing Irish jigs while shouting, "Steve the Druid Surfer will now repeal the laws of time!" and even though the models and gangbangers just ignored him—they'd seen weirder shit in LA, I suppose—my sister said, "Hang on a minute," walked straight to "Steve," removed his mask, kissed him gently on the cheek, then told him, "Repeal *that*."

VOYEURISM, REVERSED

While fucking doggy-style in Ann's completely glass-walled bedroom, we could see into the kitchen of the small ranch house next door, where a couple were eating their dinner, and this couple looked so cozy—far more than *we* felt with each other—that our fucking began to slow and finally stop and now we watched them from Ann's bed, saying nothing, not even touching, as that couple finished their meal, spoke for a while, then washed the dirty dishes together.

HERE'S ONE FOR THE MOTORHEADS

Of course we considered it astonishing to find the rusted frame of a 1939 Ford Sedan in a stream deep in the forest, with vivid greenery growing out from it—*How on earth did this thing get here?*—but even stranger was our discovery of the Ford's shattered windshield near an oak tree farther on, and then a tire farther still, and then a fender, then a door, each part appearing every few feet as if some automotive Big Bang had blown the car up, spewing not-so-stellar matter in each direction.

STRAWBERRY (2)

To you, the unsmiling old Cuban gangster with the acne-pocked and knife-scarred face and dead brown eyes and thinning Brylcreemed hair who kept staring like a wolf at my young wife from your table near ours at that Little Havana cafe; you, the gangster who ignored me as I nodded politely to you and who only left the place after slurping down your strawberry milkshake and then muttering "Vamos" to your bodyguards:

As a fellow fan of strawberry milkshakes, sir, and as a fan of my humble existence, I wish to thank you, sir, for not killing me and kidnapping my wife.

BABYLON, DC (VIVA LARRY FRANKEL)

What a taxi ride that was, crossing our nation's capital while the driver told us of how he'd once owned DC's biggest escort service;

and how a distinguished US Senator asked to sleep with three women at once but then added, "You know what? Send me a boy, too";

and how a KGB colonel fell so hard for a new escort named Velma that he defected;

and how one night at the escort service's townhouse five G-men paid for an orgy and grudgingly allowed three CIA agents to join in;

and how the service evaded a "no prostitution" policy at local hotels by starting a pizza delivery business in which you paid two hundred dollars for your mushroom pie but the delivery person stuck around to satisfy your other appetites;

and how the service's most popular escort was a seventy-two-year-old woman whom all the congresspeople and supreme court justices and cabinet secretaries fondly called (though some were even older than she was) "Grandma."

MISREADINGS

Pryna often misread bumper stickers and book titles, with "ORIGAMI FOR THE ENTHUSIAST" becoming "*ORGASMS FOR THE ENTHUSIAST*," and "I'D RATHER BE QUILTING SOMETHING" becoming "I'D RATHER BE *GUILTING SOMEONE*," but Pryna's poor vision reached its nadir (in fact, she finally vowed to start wearing glasses) when she drove past a "DEAF CHILD IN AREA" street sign, misread it as "*DEAD CHILD IN AREA*," and got scared stiff by a young boy dozing in a hammock.

Because you lived alone in that white house with blue shutters, you were baffled, of course, and frightened, by the appearance of graffiti in your bathroom—first, on one wall there, someone (*A burglar*, you figured, *or a ghost*) wrote "FOR A DEEP SUCK, CALL 736-5039"; then, the next day, on another wall they wrote "TRAPPED? MASTURBATE" (*Like most graffiti writers*, you figured, *this ghost or burglar must be a pervert*), and on it went, and each time you found a new graffito, a new black-Magic Markered mystery, the more frantic you felt, and the more *constipated*, too, since you apparently lost the ability to defecate as soon as this madness started, but today, *oh happy day*, something inside you must have come unplugged, so you rushed right to your bathroom and, *hallelujah*, out it came, days' worth of it, and as you reached for the toilet paper, you glimpsed a new one on the door facing you, a graffito that read "IN SPITE OF WHAT JUST HAPPENED, YOU'RE STILL FULL OF SHIT," which instead of troubling you made you laugh and soon feel grateful, grateful for this crazy unseen company, grateful you don't have to feel so damned alone.

63

GOT "CARBO-HIGH-DRATES" IF YOU WANT 'EM

A few years back, there was a restaurant, The Gip Sam Noodle Pride, where Pryna, a certified pasta enthusiast, would get her fix of lo mein, chow fun, udon, soba, ramen, gnocchi, fusilli, risotto, "Viennese Lamb Pad Thai," even spaetzle, on a daily basis, but a week after law enforcement shut down the joint (none of the regular customers were informed why), Pryna fell ill with nausea and stomach cramps and scorching fever, and she only found out the reason for her malady when the local paper ran this item: "Police in Hollywood revealed today that they are searching for the owners of the 'Gip Sam' noodle restaurant, three men who allegedly boosted their business by lacing all their food with opium."

GOT KIDNAP INSURANCE IF YOU WANT IT

While waiting on a long TSA line in Denver, a middle-aged businessman who stood behind me said, "It could be worse, this could be the airport in Zembla, where you need to buy 'kidnap insurance' as soon as you arrive, using your credit card in this machine they've got that looks like an ATM except it *gives* you a PIN number instead of takes one, then you walk out of the terminal and you get kidnapped, no exceptions, and don't call for the cops, cause they won't help you, they'll turn a blind eye, and so will whatever local security team your company's hired for you, they all know not to interfere (either they've been paid off or they're scared, probably both), and when the kidnappers hold a knife to your throat you tell them your new PIN number and, once it checks out, they let you go, no hard feelings, you're on your way"—and when I asked this businessman, "What happens if you risk it and *don't* buy that insurance?," he chuckled and said, "Oh, then they kill you, no hard feelings, but no exceptions, because they *have to*, it's Economics 101, if they don't kill you then the next Westerner who shows up might also bypass their product, and *then* where would these small-scale capitalists be?"

A LOCKED SAFE FULL OF AUTUMN LEAVES

There once was a woman who never dreamed and she grew so disturbed by this condition that a Maltese herbalist gave her gold pills that brought on dreams each night thereafter, Technicolor dreams that soon came true, or at least seemed so realistic that she now moved through a twilight world of utter strangeness, a world into which she finally vanished, leaving behind an empty bed.

LEGS

"At least you survived it in one piece," Pryna told her trail guide in the Monteverde Cloud Forest after he'd recounted how a bite from a viper had hospitalized him for seven weeks, weeks of paralysis and blindness and great pain, but on hearing her polite words, the guide used his walking stick to tap his calf, which made a hollow plastic sound, and then he said, "Not quite *one* piece, no."

(LET'S HAVE A) GENE POOL PARTY

Imagine you're giving a lecture where the audience members are all your ancestors, most of them oddly-dressed unfamiliar people who just stare at each other, baffled—and yet within this group will occur some lovely reunions, for instance, "So *you're* little Masha, oh, my, how *old* you've gotten, you must be older even than *me*, I can't believe it, you look so different, but I still recognize your eyes, so come *here*, dumpling, give a kiss to your Grandma Anya, who always put sweets in your hand when your stupid father wasn't watching."

BUY ME SOME STARDUST

"Can I watch that first kiss with my third wife one more time?" the dying man asked the Grim Reaper as his life finished unspooling before his eyes, and after the Reaper obliged him (which was against policy, but so what?), the last words of the man, who wasn't known in his lifetime for much politeness, were a very sincere, "Thank you."

TEARS ARE ROUND, THE SEA IS DEEP, ROLL THEM OVERBOARD AND SLEEP

Puzzled as to why people kept walking into the apartment building above the Plotz-A-Million Deli and then emerging from it only five minutes later, I asked some of them, "What's going *on* up there?" but no one answered, they all just anxiously scurried off, so I decided to investigate, climbing the staircase to the top floor, where a ceiling-mounted camera filmed me as I approached a red-haired woman who stood outside her apartment with her latest five-minute visitor, and I asked them, "You having a party?" but she just shot me a frightened look and pulled her guest inside with her and slammed her door, so I gave up and left the building and didn't think of this mystery again until weeks later when I read in our local tabloid about a murder in that apartment—the redhead I'd spoken to was a hashish dealer who'd been shot to death by two customers who were soon identified by that camera in the hallway—and now the Plotz-A-Million Deli is gone but that apartment is probably still there and that hallway camera may still be there, too, watching the living come and go and maybe even the dead, as well, ghosts like that dealer who might be standing outside her home now, puzzled by her lack of customers, unaware that she's out of business.

FIND THE LEVEE, BURN IT DOWN

"Nice, ordinary guy" was my opinion of Anselm Schnitzky when I met him at a *seder*, unaware that he'd saved himself when he was a child by hiding out in a Ukrainian forest, dodging nightly Nazi sweeps, foraging for food with friends, watching his cousin die of typhus, watching his aunt succumb to madness, and giving directions to a wounded Russian soldier who came running to the boy one rainy day and yelled, "Quick, kid, point me to where the Germans are, I want to kill some before this chest wound does me in."

HALLELUJAH, I'M READY TO GO

Please allow me to introduce the saint Edwige Carboni (1880–1952), who was taught by the Virgin to turn all Communists to God, who brought along her guardian angel when she went shopping (he'd wait invisibly outside each store), and who was joined by Jesus once while she did laundry, her Lord pretending to help by hand but actually directing Edwige's clothes to wash and dry and fold themselves.

CLEAR RECEPTION

In a different version of your life, your father fails to protect your head from being struck by a baseball during batting practice at Yankee Stadium in 1970, which will leave his arm unbroken but leave you brain-damaged and living in a clinic where your parents visit each week, and though the nurses call you "No-One-Home" because you never move or talk or do much else, the truth is you're in a constant state of bliss, a clear receiver, with every sight and sound and smell and taste and faint sensation on your skin making you feel utterly ecstatic.

THE JACK STORY

One night not long before she lost her life, Marilyn Monroe bumped into her friend Jack and told him, "That advice you gave me three years ago when we went shopping has helped me so much," and Jack laughed, saying, "I'm glad to hear it," but then Marilyn frowned and said, "I can tell by your face you don't remember what the advice was," and even though Jack told her that *of course* he remembered, the truth is, he'd forgotten it, and for the long six decades left to him, he kept trying to identify that advice he'd given Marilyn, as if his remembering it, however too late, could retroactively somehow save her.

MY WEAKNESS
IS NONE OF YOUR BUSINESS (1)

Old Ulrich was a drunk, prone to passing out and sleeping in public places, and one day in his village, a local boy boarded a bus and put a knife to the driver's throat and made the passengers exit the vehicle so he could drive to his ex-girlfriend's house and ram the bus right into it, but after scaring some pedestrians, he crashed the bus into a streetlamp, which knocked him out, and when the police climbed on board to arrest the boy, assuming the bus was empty, they heard Old Ulrich, who'd slept through everything, still snoring loudly in the back seat.

THE AMERICAN MYSTERY DEEPENS

While waiting in the line at my local post office, I noticed a new employee, a skinny young acne'd man whose name tag read "Ray," and because this clerk appeared to be the same guy, "Raymond Eugene Harding" who was "Being Sought for Armed Robbery" in a Most Wanted poster on the wall (I never fail to give those things a close look), I wondered, as I stood face-to-face with Ray, why he worked *here*, of all places: was he casing the place for a new crime, or was that Most Wanted notice some kind of in-house joke, or could Ray simply not find another job?

I never realized that I was alive, never truly *got* it, until the summer night in Buenos Aires when I sat at a outdoor café and three burly men who stood near me began to argue, and then my fellow customers knocked over their tables and ducked behind them and I saw that the burly men were holding pistols, meaning that the firecrackers I heard now were actually gunshots (*Shit, these guys are shooting at each other!*), so I panicked, of course, but instead of ducking behind my table (*What if one of these shooters shows up to finish me off while I'm cowering down there?*), I just made a run for it, leaving my backpack behind and losing the Birkenstock sandal from my right foot as I leaped over a low stone wall, and I cut up that foot pretty badly as I ran but I hardly noticed this because my mind was too focused on the chance that I'd feel hot lead in my back at any moment, and I grimaced—I guess you'd call it "a rictus grin"—when I ran past a tiny Indian girl who'd pressed herself against the side of a brick building, and the look on her face was so calm that I thought, *She must consider me a coward, running scared like this*, and half a block away I hailed a taxi and jumped inside it but I was so breathless by now that I couldn't tell the driver what had happened, and besides I was in shock and couldn't think of any Spanish, so I just made the shape of a pistol with my right hand and said, "*Plaza Dorrego, bang-bang-bang*" and the driver's eyes lit up as he said, "*Sí?*" but by now I'd noticed that the gunfire had stopped and I thought about my abandoned backpack, so I jumped out of that taxi, ignoring the driver's curses, and hobbled on my still-sandaled left foot and my bloody bare right foot back to the café, where one of the burly men lay dead and another one lay wounded, calling in a deep voice for his mother, and, alas, my backpack was gone—someone said the café waiter had stolen it as soon as the shooting ended—but I didn't care about that because, quite simply, I felt *high*, higher than I'd ever felt before, and all my senses were buzzing and everything glowed with a smeared white inner light, so I just hobbled around in circles, thinking, *I'm alive, I really am*, and when I heard a voice call "*Señor*," I turned and saw that tiny calm-faced Indian girl standing now beside the low stone wall I'd leaped over, and when I said, "*Sí?*, she pointed to a patch of ground beside her, and once my eyes followed her finger, *yes*, there it was, right where it fell off of my right foot: that forgotten Birkenstock sandal (which, alas, I'd lose forever on a beach in Uruguay the following week).

SYNAGOGUE TIME TRAVEL

We realized that our rabbi had finally lost it at Zurskin's funeral when, nearing ninety, the rabbi began his eulogy with praise for Zurskin as "a pillar of our synagogue for many decades," but he soon grew mixed-up and spoke of the dead man as "this fine *Bar Mitzvah* boy, so full of promise," and on the rabbi went in this vein until two pallbearers stood and with great gentleness stopped his talk and led him slowly to his seat.

THE WHEEL HAS TURNED AND I AM HERE

Karl's daughter assumed what everyone assumed, that the truck had struck Karl on his Vespa by accident and that the last word he'd uttered, overheard by a witness as Karl lay shattered on the highway—the word "*idiot*"—had been directed at the truck driver (as in, "*You're an idiot for driving so badly*"), but when the trucker testified that it was *Karl* who'd slammed into *him* ("came right at me," is how he put it), Karl's daughter remembered how depressed Karl had been feeling lately and she remembered, too, having heard that suicides often regret their fatal decision before they die, so now she saw that the "idiot" her father spoke of may well have been himself.

THE BALLAD OF COCO AND CALVIN

The left side of her face was lovely, the right side had been shattered in a car crash; she was Austin's best-liked party promoter; and one night she told me, "Come meet my new beau, he's a cowboy singer, just the sexiest guy since Errol Flynn (who my mother claims she dated), he lost his US record deal but he's still *huge* in Europe, with French girls tossing their panties at him whenever he plays the Olympia"—so she drove us to a shack where her boyfriend turned out to be a broken-looking old man, like Willie Nelson if Willie took too many wrong turns, but when he sat on his food-stained sofa and sang and played guitar, she gazed at him with a love that shone from both sides of her face, and the next time I went to Paris, I saw his own face on a poster that read, "Returning Soon to the Olympia."

THE HEART OF A CHAMPION

At the hotel bar Map started speaking with two young sisters from São Paolo, his ardor focused on the older one until her boyfriend showed up, at which point Map's ardor shifted to the younger, who boasted to him that back home she was a martial arts champion, and later that night Map and this champ went swimming together in the hotel pool where, as Map stepped forward in the shallow end to embrace her, she grabbed his arms and twisted them and put him into a jujitsu hold with her knee pressed in his back, positioned well to snap his spine, and as he pleaded with her to stop, she said, "I only stop if you admit you like my sister more than me, you find her more sexy than me, you wish you swim with *her*, not *me—admit it, gringo!*"

STEAM

It was his first time outside Tanzania, this boy who'd flown alone to the Netherlands for a football scholarship, but as soon as he left the airport terminal, looking for a bus that would bring him to his hostel in the Hague, everything went wrong: not only was the air colder than anything he could have imagined (his sponsor had failed to warn him it was winter here) but every time he exhaled, parts of his soul left his mouth in the form of gray steam, so he shouted in Swahili to everyone around him, "*Something is wrong, I must be dying, please help me, people!*" —and when they didn't come to his aid, the boy wished he'd learned Dutch, even just a few words, as his cousin had advised him.

LESSONS FROM THE DRUNK TANK

Sure, I learned some lessons the night I spent in the Santa Barbara County Jail, including the big existential one in which I realized how fragile my physical freedom is—*I've been kidnapped by the* police, I kept thinking, amazed that the people who were supposed to maintain such freedom were the same ones who'd now snatched it from me—but the most useful lesson concerned the "drunk tank," and how, as soon as I beheld it, this filthy cage with sneering men and a broken toilet, I froze with fright and whispered to the cop who'd led me there, "Officer, I'm just a college kid from Long Island, that place doesn't look *safe* for me," and I believed I saw some mercy begin to stir in his gray eyes until he shouted (oh, that mustard-scented breath), "*SHUT THE FUCK UP!*"—and then straight into my new home he shoved me.

ROSES TO DEADEN THE CLODS AS THEY FALL

My uncle Wolf said, "Viewing the cave paintings at Lascaux was not emotional for me—fascinating, but not *emotional*— until I noticed that, of all the hand-prints on the walls there, a few artists favored their left hands, and *this* is what ultimately touched me, what made me feel close to those prehistoric people: like my sister, who's now as dead as they are, some of them were lefties."

ONE COLD VIBE WON'T STOP
THIS HERE BOOGIE

My father, a radar operator on fighter planes in World War II, told me he never felt frightened by turbulence on a commercial aircraft, and when I asked, "Not even a little?" he just shook his head and said, "I'll worry about going down once we *start* going down, not before."

LIFTOFF WITH AYSHEA

A lovable old Swede who was a friend of my family, Nina could predict the future with a pack of playing cards—she'd foreseen my mother's death by this method—and Nina once told me, "When I was a girl, an old Gypsy woman in a fur coat beckoned to me at Stockholm's Central Station, saying, 'I sense you have the same power I have, so I shall tell you how old you shall be when you die, you shall be *eighty*,'" but Nina ended up living to ninety-one, which made the Gypsy's prediction wrong—unless we consider that at eighty Nina sank into dementia.

STORY COMPOSED OUTSIDE THE RUINS OF THE NEVELE HOTEL

First, they ran out of toilet paper in the Toilet Museum's bathroom, leaving me in quite a pickle; *then* I slipped and fell inside the Tort Law Museum's foyer, then smashed my head on the Geology Museum's new exhibit, then got ripped off by the P. T. Barnum Museum's cashier, then suffered an asthma attack in the Proust Museum's bathroom (where they also had zero toilet paper); and *now*, after all that, you really expect me to go with you to the Leprosy Museum?

THE WHAMMY, CLEVELAND STYLE

The kid said, "My mother's a witch, so if you're not good boyfriend material, she'll turn you into a camel and sell you to the Cleveland Zoo, where for eight years kids will throw stones at your hump while their fathers' backs are turned, and then, even once you're you again—I mean, restored to human form—you'll still need to wait around in town till Mama gives you a second chance."

CHOCOLATE (1)

"Where's your mother?" the friendly Indian owner of the Häagen-Dazs store in Livingston would ask whenever he handed me my weekly Chocolate Fudge cone, but instead of saying, "She died" (who wanted to go through *that* tale with this near-stranger?), I always said, "Oh, she's at home, I'll tell her you said hi," and this went on until the ice cream man just stopped mentioning my mother, which I felt glad about at first but soon regretted, because I saw now that by telling the ice cream man, "My mother's at home," I was keeping her alive for one last person who'd sort of known her.

WHIRL IS KING

First my reading of a W. G. Sebald novel on the subway platform got interrupted by a male lunatic shouting, "Dirty deeds done dirt cheap," then my Sebald reading got interrupted again by a female lunatic screaming wordlessly, as if in response to the first lunatic, then my Sebald reading got interrupted yet again when the train roared into the station and I glanced up from page six just in time to watch a sad-faced, orange-coated old man—perhaps another lunatic in this pocket of lunacy-tinged New York—leap right onto the tracks beneath those unforgiving wheels, and I remember how everybody shrieked at once, and I remember how blank the first two lunatics' faces now looked—they plainly felt as harrowed as did the rest of us—and I remember waking up the following morning to learn of a car wreck that had killed the writer Sebald the night before.

NATHAN RIGOLETTI HAS RISEN FROM THE GRAVE!

Up through New Jersey earth he clawed, then he went running along the Turnpike, a click-clacking skeleton shaking worms off his bones and spitting soil from his mouth, and once he found Jill in her high-rise Brooklyn co-op, which she'd paid for with her inheritance, Nathan ripped the brand-new yin-yang off her shoulder, shouting, "Tattoos are for *hippies*, not for any daughter of mine!"

FULL CHICKEN REALNESS

The only restaurant still open in this sleepy Zemblan town was a bistro where I ordered the daily special, "Chicken Francese," but when the dish at last arrived, the meat bore the flavor, color, and consistency of cardboard, so I complained to the manager, "This doesn't taste quite like chicken" and he answered, "Oh, you want *real* chicken—well, no, sorry, we used up all our *real* chicken for a funeral reception we catered yesterday."

HOOK-MOON

Our journey by dirigible was only supposed to last two hours—"The Tourist Special" is how they billed it—but our captain abandoned ship when he heard his wife was cheating, and once his parachute deployed, we turned our spyglass to other marvels we drifted over, and oh, what a Grand Voyage this turned into!—although with time we started fearing we'd never see our homes again, and just before we lost all hope, we came upon a floating city, a city built on clouds, the so-called "drowned city" of Atlantis—"Although," its viceroy said, "we never sank into the sea, that was just gossip, no, Zeus *adored* us, and with his aid (as well as bleeding-edge technology) we raised ourselves up to the sky, far from the ignorance displayed by non-Atlanteans"—and as the viceroy and his valets helped us from our ship and we found that this *terra firma* was rather *squishy*, as you'd expect cloud-land would be, I glanced up at the moon, a yellow hook-moon, its points so sharp they'd poke your eyes out if you gazed at them for too long.

SHORTIES: A SALMAGUNDI WITH HURRICANE DROPS

The Gnostics tell us that a false god burned down our world, so is this why, Joanne, that you always taste like ashes?

✳

I couldn't believe how sweet my friend's dog Phoebe was—obviously pit bulls had gotten a bad rap!—but when I mentioned this to him, he said, "Tell that to the German Shepherd Phoebe slaughtered."

✳

Poleaxed by a long night drinking absinthe, the sybarite got up to pee, started reading the Sunday *New York Times,* and finished the first three sections before remembering the eager naked woman he'd left behind in his waterbed.

✳

The hostility between Fran and her son-in-law was so open and so deep for so long—"I wish that loser had never been *born*" went Fran's usual refrain—that her nine-year-old granddaughter finally said, "You know, Grandma, if Daddy never got born, then *I* would've never got born, *either,*" so Fran hugged the girl to her and cooed, "Oh, my darling, I love you *so* much—but forgive me, I'd make that trade."

✳

"No, of *course* you can't name our new puppy 'Hitler,'" Daddy told Donnie, shooting the boy an angry look, "because then all the kikes and spooks and fucking faggots will poison it when we're not looking."

✳

While we watched the Grim Reaper take his lunch break in Luna Park, with that toothless mouth of his working away at a ham sandwich, my child turned to me and asked, "Do you think Death likes his job, Dad?"

⸝⸝⸜⸜

At a glitzy show-business party a woman asked a famous actor who was nearly twice her age, "Wanna dance?" and his reply was, "Wrong *verb*, baby, that's the wrong *verb*"—but in *my* version of this story the woman puts him in his place by saying, "We're all fools, '*baby*', whether we dance or not—so we might as well dance."

⸝⸝⸜⸜

"Finally I realized," said the seventy-year-old woman who sat near Pryna on the tour bus in Tallinn, "that you can't change other people, you can only change yourself, so after years of being mistreated by my husband and my son, I packed my bags and took our car and drained our joint bank account and haven't spoken to them since."

⸝⸝⸜⸜

I wouldn't mind having a threesome with them, Map thinks about the beautiful couple he's just met (the guy forty-eight, his girlfriend nineteen), but all desire drains out of Map here in this groovy Rotterdam bar when he asks the woman, "How long have you been together?" and with no discernible shame she answers, "Eight years—his daughter was my friend in primary school."

⸝⸝⸜⸜

"My secret," said the painter of realistic lion pictures, "is to always show these babes roaring so you won't notice how bad I am at drawing paws."

⁓⁓⁓

"Instinct being what it is, I'll bet they didn't mourn for long," my wife remarked as we watched the pair of wild geese do their daily walk across our lawn—this pair left alone now since a local fox had snatched their chicks—and I hated that fox for what it did until a few days later when I watched it run down our street, its eyes ablaze with such raw vitality that I thought, *Okay, this* one *time I'll forgive you.*

⁓⁓⁓

One of your strangest blind dates was with a man who said, "I don't like watching movies or TV shows because I'm afraid that the characters onscreen will one day turn to look at me—*me*, sitting in that cinema or living room!—and begin to scrutinize my behavior just as I've been scrutinizing theirs."

⁓⁓⁓

Sarka's mother didn't want another baby, but the morning she was scheduled for an abortion, Soviet tanks rolled into Prague, shutting down everything, health clinics included, which led to outrage, turmoil, a doomed violent resistance, and Sarka.

⁓⁓⁓

Right before the Nazi guard machine-guns the prisoners, Robert Desnos, the only poet among them, pretends to read his neighbor's palm, telling her triumphantly, "Two more children for you and a long life," and then he reads more sunny futures in the many offered palms, leading the doomed to grow so hopeful, and so unruly, that their murders get postponed... until tomorrow.

At Pryna's law school she received poor grades on her first report card, mostly C's and D's, which upset her, of course, until she bumped into her classmate Bo, who was kicking a wall and shouting "*Fuck*," and when she said to him, "Guess you did lousy *too*, huh?," secretly delighted because misery loves company, of course, Bo said, "Damn *right* I did lousy—I got a fucking *B*!"

How excruciating I found it to gaze into the vitrine at the Scary Creatures exhibit in Rio where a hairy tarantula rested, utterly patient—it would feed when it was ready, not until— and writhing helplessly beside it was a hairless knuckle-sized pink mouse fetus that seemed to understand only too well how much its brief future would suck.

Yes, you've had fevers in your day, plenty of fevers—"breakbone," "parrot," "jungle," "white-line," and even, a few times, "cat-scratch"—but in your experience, no fever will last as long as the kind sung about by Peggy Lee.

The taxi driver kept wondering, *What's this humming sound that's coming from my backseat?* until his passenger there, a well-dressed woman in her seventies who'd been speaking calmly on her cellphone with a friend, began to gasp loudly and he realized that she'd been busy all the while with a vibrator.

Map said, "I can't stop thinking about Hank Williams getting chauffeured around while he lay dead in the back seat of his Cadillac," so Pryna said, "That ride only sealed the deal, hon, Hank *truly* died eight months earlier when he and his friend Minnie Pearl were singing his song 'I Saw The Light' and Hank suddenly stopped, looking terrified, and said, 'I can't see no light, Minnie—there *ain't* no light...'"

〜〜〜

"I'm never jealous," she used to boast, but at the orgy her younger lover grew too enamored of other women so she got dressed and went home early, taking with her the lover's wallet, cellphone, clothing, ski jacket, and snow boots, which meant he had to walk home naked in a blizzard.

〜〜〜

86   Your boyfriend's constant snores keep you awake at night until you learn to comprehend the secrets his snoring nose convey, secrets that include his weekly visits to a prostitute called "the Torpedo," the money he embezzled from his last job, the night he struck a puppy with his Nissan, and—yes, *this*, as well—the boundless love he feels for you.

〜〜〜

Among the many reasons why I'm fond of the 1971 movie *Harold and Maude* is the fact that, according to *Box Office Magazine*, a young man named Doug Strand saw the film 122 times in its first year of release, which I find touching because of how ardent Strand's need obviously was—and how he was able to fill that need, again and again and again.

〜〜〜

In a dream you met God, who explained, "My hands are hands of loving-kindness—hands of fate in a pleasant mood," and as you exhaled, relieved by this report, God added, as if you might as well know the whole score, "But when I jerk off, keeping those hands otherwise occupied, some really bad shit might happen to you."

ᴧᴧᴧᴧᴧᴧ

Map went to see a psychic once, a total stranger, and her first remark was, "Just so you know I'm for real, let me say that eight and eighteen play big roles in your life," which was true, but being skeptical about psychics, Map tested her by saying, "No, those numbers mean nothing to me," and she looked briefly puzzled before she pointed to her door and said, "You're toying with me—*get out.*"

ᴧᴧᴧᴧᴧᴧ

"Of all the recordings you've made, which is the best?" I asked Udo, the renowned German klezmer musician, and his response was, "I never compare any one thing to another—I just listen to each recording of mine and think, *That's where I was* that *year.*

ᴧᴧᴧᴧᴧᴧ

At the Pukersdorf asylum we cure the patients with the sound of running water, gentle, lapping, gurgling sounds broadcast to each room, but for the troublemakers, we've built an apparatus that holds large stones above their heads, water-smoothed stones that will fall and cause concussions if those shit-stirrers drift asleep and lose their grip on the cord that keeps the stones raised.

ᴧᴧᴧᴧᴧᴧ

At a bookstore in Sioux City where a sweet-faced man, a fellow shopper, had advised me which trail guide to buy, I started flipping through a paperback about a local serial killer, and this book contained a photo of the killer's last would-be victim, a sweet-faced man—the one and same, yes—who'd turned the tables on the killer by fighting back, despite a stab wound, and strangling that killer to death.

⁂

The legend goes that every New Year's Eve, an angel rises from Lake Hopatcong to ask the first person it meets, "Does Gary Lippman still worry too much about what people think of him?" and when the answer is, as always, "Of course he does," the angel shakes its head and then descends into the lake for another year.

LATE FLOWERING

When Pryna told the middle-aged blonde in a business suit and the Balinese college student who was stroking the blonde's thigh, "Forgive me, but you two seem like, well, an unconventional couple," they both laughed at that Reno bar and then the college student said, "It's true we don't have much in common, but she's my mistress and I'm her slave and I've been living in the dungeon in her duplex."

POWER: LESSON 18

Because they both knew that the person who cares *less* about the other in any relationship has more power, Joyce and Frank each chose to numb themselves, and so down their feelings spiraled, down, down, down as in a whirlpool, until that couple disappeared, leaving behind a marriage license, some photo albums, a blue tuxedo, a bridal gown, a plain gold band, a diamond ring—oh, and a frightened girl named Betty.

THE CLAW OF THE SEA-PUSS WILL GET US ALL IN THE END

Pryna never really thought about the phrase *"so close yet so far"* until the night when she was strolling north on Broadway and a crazed man appeared beside her waving a handgun in her face and hissing, "I'm gonna *shoot* that cop, he fucked my *sister*, I'm gonna *kill* him," and even though Pryna could make eye contact with the people walking past her, her gaze imploring each stranger, *"Help me,"* they saw her plight and kept their distance, as if to say, "Yes, we share this sidewalk with you, but we're on a different planet—a planet with no madmen, guns, cops, or sisters."

FREAKY SUCKAGE

What a weird blind date that was, with Vesna acting hostile from the start and saying, "So I guess your life is *fucked*" when I mentioned my mother died, and then, while we sat in her Volvo after dinner, she declined to let me kiss her but began unbuttoning her blouse, tugged down one bra cup, and held her left breast out to me, saying in a baby voice, "Here, little boy-boy, suck Mommy's titty, you know you want to, so don't be scared, just come on, *suck*," and even though I thought, *This woman's nuts*, a moment later I was on her, moaning "Mommy," pleading "Mommy," and sucking that thing as if it held my sole salvation.

THE CONJURED WORLD

So, after eight months, she's begun to smile again, and she's even gone back to her job at Fern Gardens, but on those nights when she declines to join her friends for dinners or parties, telling them, "I'm staying home; I'm just too tuckered out to socialize," she goes alone to see a movie, something for children, and as she watches, she tries to guess which parts her dead boy would have liked best.

A PIRATE'S LIFE FOR ASHER

The boy who almost lost his virginity on Yom Kippur in the cloakroom of a synagogue, where his seducer, an older girl, had used some stranger's fur coat to serve as their bed but the boy came even before he made it inside her, prompting the girl to frown at the pricey, now soiled coat and say, "You made *a big mess*, Asher"—that boy grew up and changed his name to "Andrew" and lived a pirate's life, making new messes, all kinds of messes, as he gambled and swindled and robbed and (oh, most disreputable work of all!) became a actor, and in his eighties we got to be friends and soon I liked him as though I'd known him for much longer, and last night when he died, I thought, *All your messes, Asher, such big and wild messes, but they aged better than a non-pirate's proper wins.*

ONCE, TWICE, THREE TIMES A LYCANTHROPE

"Lycanthropic Larry" was a hairdresser by day and a *bon vivant* by night—except for full-moon nights when he shed his clothes, grabbed some glue as well as grooming scissors, dashed out of his salon, and ran around till dawn seeking victims with fluffy hair, after which he'd wake up beneath a tree in Central Park, bloodstained and smelly and wondering why all this *fur* was stuck to his bare chest.

THIS STORY IS A MACHINE FOR EXORCISING A GHOST

There's a Greek saying that if you turn your back on love, your luck will turn against you, which makes me think of Caroline—Caroline, the woman I knew just for a month during our second year at college but began to fall in love with and might have *stayed* in love with, too, had I not asked her one day in our dining hall, "Why do you cut your hair so short?" and she said, "Well, to reveal that, can I trust you?" and I laughed, saying, "Sure," so she said, "It's not actually my real hair, it's a wig, I lost my real hair from chemotherapy, I had breast cancer," and for a moment I just stared at her, too stunned to speak, staring and thinking of my mother who'd died of the same thing two years before, but I listened as Caroline told me about her illness, which was now in remission, and when she finished I hugged her and pretended all was well, and yet it wasn't, everything had changed, because now I thought, *Death's stalking me, snatching everyone I care about—first my mother and soon, if her own cancer comes back, this college sophomore*—and so I pulled away from Caroline, still pretending all was well but beginning to avoid her, saying I was busy, too busy to ever meet, and she must have recognized my distance for what it was although she never called me on it, all she did was smile sadly as I ran through my latest lame excuse, and I hated how I was acting, how I was turning my back on love, but I couldn't stop this disappearing act, I just could not allow myself to grow close to one more (possibly) dying person, and by the time the summer came, she and I were hardly speaking, and there was silence all that summer, and come the autumn she had not come back to school, she'd either dropped out or transferred elsewhere or—*no*, I couldn't bear to think of *that*, and so I worried about

92

Caroline but not enough, not nearly enough, and if my luck does turn at last, I think I'll know why, and yet I wish now, forty years on, that I could meet her one more time and hear her say, "You didn't hurt me all that much, because I realized, even then, how scared, and weak, and *young* you were."

GUNPOWDER ON HIS BREATH

Intrigued by Melvin's homemade hat, which spelled out "Youngest Living Veteran Of World War II," I approached him and asked about it in the bookstore in Missoula where we were browsing, and he explained that he'd "knocked up" a married woman in his hometown when he was twelve ("I looked eighteen, or even older"), and so the judge gave him a choice—jailhouse or army—and Melvin said, "Easy, your Honor, praise the Lord and please pass me the ammunition."

BE MY BRENDA 8

Over the years, I received some strangely personal fortune cookie messages at Gip Sam Noodle Pride (*before my first time masturbating*: "Give your love a guiding hand"; *before losing my virginity*: "Be as hard as you can or as soft as you must be"; and *before breaking up with a girlfriend*: "You love her as much as you can, but you do not love her enough"), but the strangest fortune cookie message I've gotten read, "Inspected by Brenda 8," which prompted me to wonder whether this "Brenda 8" was my future bride, or else the woman who'd someday give me syphilis, or someone else important, and when I discovered what the message actually was—*not* a fortune, after all, but the quality-control tag from a pair of cotton men's briefs, which somehow found its way into my cookie—I swore, "I'll never go back to Gip Sam," although the lo mein there, which I do love, soon lured me back.

SAID THE WOMAN
WITH CROPPED GRAY HAIR

Said the woman with cropped gray hair, "Back in '47 this girl named Sarah told her new husband, a man she met after leaving Dachau, that she would never bear any children, at least not while her brother, thirteen years old, was still missing, but then one day she got a letter from another Dachau survivor, someone who'd been there with Sarah's brother and who'd watched her brother die, and the first thing Sarah did after crumpling up that letter was not to break down in tears but to run into her kitchen and grab her husband and shout at him, 'Fuck me now, Ben, let's make a baby, that's what I want, I want a baby'—and they named me Heloise."

CAKE-WALKING MONOZYGOTE FROM HOME

While watching the elderly identical twin sisters at this café—
the two of them dressed perfectly alike, speaking their own
language with each other, and ignoring everyone else—I, an
only child, wonder if they live in the same home, and if they
might even be lovers, and if they've ever had *other* lovers, and
if, should one sister learn she's dying, they would choose to
share death just how they've chosen to share their lives (if
"choice" is even the correct word).

BEWARE THE GOLEM

One of your strangest blind dates was with a woman who
devoured during a single restaurant meal one shrimp po'boy,
a big dish of beef *chow mein*, vegetarian corn hay, one shot of
Droog vodka, a rasher of lobster mac 'n' cheese, three chorizo
dumplings, an "Occam's Razor Burger," a wheel of Lipplotzer
cheese, peacock pie, plenty of kishkes and kasha, a "Postmodern
Pastrami Reuben," "Duck Surprise" with a modest palm wine
drizzle, jellied eels, a bowl of "Blind Lemon Gumbo," salad with
shark oil, an Animal Cracker–crusted catfish salad, filet mignon
with a blueberry sauce reduction, a tureen of poutine (with extra
curds), something called "Blisters on Kenny's Sister," something
else called "The Masked Tortilla," a Verka-flavored omelet (hold
the garlic and onions), Lorelei beer ("One sip," reads the label,
"and it's into the rocks you go"), a chopped-liver sculpture in the
likeness of Buddy Hackett, sour Iranian peanut brittle, one hot
tart, chocolate-covered tsetse flies, an egg cream, three Vichy
waters, fugu yoghurt, sea cucumbers, and a ginger sling with
a pineapple tart, all of it washed down with Eau de High John

Conqueror and culminating with a thirty-six-inch-high dessert called "The Golem" (although this last dish finally broke the eater, remaining unfinished)—and when you asked her if she always ate so much, she burped and said, "Better a short life with width than a narrow life with length."

THE MUSA CALLIOPE

"When you're stuck and don't know what to do," a great crime novelist once advised beginning writers who've reach an impasse in their plotting, *"have a strange woman in a trench coat crash through a window with a pistol,"* words that amused a certain author whose teenage daughter had recently died, but just last night as he was writing his new book, avoiding his grief by losing himself in another one of his hardboiled-detective novels, a woman *did* come crashing through his window, and once she'd taken off her trench coat and set her pistol on his desk, she wagged a finger at the writer and then she told him, "You're too hardboiled—why don't you write about *her* instead?"

THE TIME WE LEARN IS NOW

One night when Marlene Dietrich sang "Where Have All the Flowers Gone?" I heard the last verse for the first time—the graveyard going back to flowers, making a circle—so I decided to go back to the woman whose love I'd spurned and to meet the child we'd made together, and as I handed the woman a bouquet (as if this gift was penance enough), she started humming "Where Have All the Flowers Gone?," amazing me—and confirming, too, that I had come to the right place.

ON THE ORAL INGESTION OF DOVE SOAP

Your mother would "wash your mouth out with soap," a bar of Dove Soap, whenever you used "dirty" language, a punishment you'd remember decades later while you were going down on someone whose genitalia tasted of Dove (you'd met this person earlier that night in a loud Havana bar), and soon the Dove taste got you thinking of a story you'd once heard, the story of a crazed man who bought a bar of Dove and promptly ate it, and when the shopkeeper told him, "Soap's not used that way," the crazed man answered, "Don't tell me my business—you should see what we eat at home."

PRESIDENT CARLYLE, MARKED FOR DEATH

After my father died, I figured I'd seen the last of my wicked stepmother, but this year she got elected US president ("*Today* my gated village in Palm Springs," she used to cackle, "*tomorrow* the world!"), and now my scheme to assassinate her and thereby save our republic from this tyrant has just been thwarted by the goon squad she sent to nab me without her even knowing what I'd planned.

ANOTHER DAY IN THE LIFE OF A FOOL: A DOUBLE PLAY

Of all the pedestrians who were forced to walk around the sunburned man who lay on his back on the sidewalk munching an egg sandwich and reading a *Silver Surfer* comic book, only Map took the trouble to ask him, "Hey, what's up?" to which the man replied, "When I turned thirty, I realized I'm a fool—I'd always *been* one; I'd always *be* one—and since that day I haven't had one unhappy hour."

Of all the pedestrians who were forced to walk around the sunburned man who lay on his back on the sidewalk munching an egg sandwich and reading a *Silver Surfer* comic book, only Pryna lay herself down beside him, accepted a small bite from his sandwich, politely declined a peek at his comic book, then turned to gaze up at the sky, that big cerulean bowl where she pictured the Silver Surfer heading west.

WHICH GAME IS AFOOT? (OR, THE CASE OF THE RETIRED HOMICIDE DETECTIVE)

When it was time for the Cleveland homicide detective to retire, he was still puzzling about the Chaunce case—did a woman fatally bludgeon her college roommate, or was the culprit a serial killer who'd been spotted on campus that night?—and as the years passed, "puzzling about" turned to "obsessing," which of course upset the ex-detective's family and made him into "the second victim" (his shrink sure had a way with words), and all the while the ex-detective told himself, I can't find out if there's a God, or what life means, but if I solve this case, I'll be like Sherlock Holmes for one last time and not remembered as a failure.

ENCORE

In the nursing home TV room, where Map's father was staring blankly at a wildlife show in which a lioness chased and brought down antelopes, Map assumed that the old man, lost in dementia, had no idea what he was watching, but when the son pushed his father's wheelchair toward the door, saying, "Dinnertime, Dad—it's steak tonight," the old man moaned and shook his head and said, "Wait—just one more kill."

WHEN WISHING STILL HELPED...

Way back when wishing still helped, an evil giant swallowed a restaurant owner named Dom, who felt frightened inside the giant's belly, so Dom said, "Please also swallow my mother, she's the cook at my restaurant," and the giant obliged—it was just more food for him—but Dom soon felt the need to boss someone around, so he said, "Now please swallow my son, he's the bartender at my restaurant," and the giant again obliged, but Dom soon felt lonely, so he said, "Now please swallow my girlfriend, she's the waitress at my restaurant," and the giant again obliged, but Dom soon felt guilty about having his girlfriend there, so he said, "Now please swallow my wife, she's the bookkeeper for my restaurant," and the giant again obliged, but by this time Dom and his family realized they had nothing to eat, so Dom said, "Now please swallow our restaurant where

I recently re-stocked the pantry, it's 'Galante's' in Elizabeth, New Jersey," and the giant again obliged—although the giant had begun to feel exploited—and as soon as the family inside him had emptied their pantry, they used their knives to shave fresh meat from the giant's belly lining, so by the time they'd broken through to the world outside, the giant had perished and they built a door in the hole they'd made and put up a sign that read, "Please join us at our spacious new location."

THANATOS TRUMPING EROS

The idea tonight was to make love in the cadaver lab—*Eros trumping Thanatos!*—but as soon as Map's new girlfriend, a medical student, got them in there with her key, the smell of formaldehyde wiped out Map's libido, so he just walked, holding his nose, from corpse to corpse, astounded by each: the "fresh" young bearded man who looked asleep despite a wedge cut from his forehead, the gray-haired woman whose open eyes peered at them with what seemed like only mild curiosity, and the yellow featureless pile of sludge that bewildered Map—just what *was* it?—until his girlfriend said, "That former person is the epitome of *not-fresh*."

WHAT FOOLS WE WERE
TO SIGN UP FOR TIME

As a teenager she heard the wisdom in the Rolling Stones' lyric "*What a drag it is growing old*," and so she decided to keep from aging—it wasn't easy, but she did it, and in time she drew encouragement from some new words by the Stones, "*Don't you think it's sometimes wise not to grow old?*" (actually, they sang "*grow* up" and not "*grow* old," but she heard what she wanted to hear), and for decades she remained young despite her loved ones nagging her, urging her to "act her age," to *be* her age ("The Stones are *grandfathers* now," they said), and in the end all of that pressure wore her out, so she gave up and let time win, she let it wrinkle her and shrink her, and for a while, too, she felt content to be so old, but now she understands she's blown it, betrayed herself, because today here at the Peaceful Waters Rest Home she's opened up a book of Hasid wisdom and the first words her eyes have settled on are "It is forbidden to grow old."

BACHELORETTE

As soon as the drunk young man in leather pants climbed out of the window in Pryna's ninth-floor San Francisco hotel room and stood dancing on the ledge there with a Michelob in one hand and a Camel in the other, she understood that if he fell, she might get blamed for pushing him (she'd only opened that window, anyway, because he wanted to smoke before they fucked), and when Pryna pleaded with this man to come back in, all he did was laugh and keep on dancing, and when he suddenly stumbled and dropped his cigarette and beer while grabbing onto the window frame to save himself, Pryna sank back onto her bed with a gasp, suffering what may well have been her life's first heart attack and thinking to herself (although she may have said it out loud), *"I don't want to be single anymore."*

IF YOU HAVE GHOSTS, THEN YOU HAVE EVERYTHING

"I thought you're upstairs sleeping," says the woman to her husband who's just appeared beside her near their home as she walks their dog, and, smiling wistfully, he says, "I *was*, but then I died from a stroke in bed, I never woke up, don't be scared, and yes, I know how we agreed that whoever goes first won't come back to visit—'Let the survivor get on with life,' is what we said, 'no ghostly appearances, no corny closure'—but I stopped here to say goodbye because I know now that you'll *need* it, this loving final word from me."

THERE'S A LAW, THERE'S AN ARM, THERE'S A HAND

Not long before your friend Gray was convicted of financial chicanery and then got cut down by a hit-and-run driver, which left him too damaged to go to prison, he told you over dinner at his favorite Santa Fe nightclub, "My role model is my mother, a nurse who slipped on ice outside our home when I was ten and broke her arm, but because she knew this injury would not be covered by Workmen's Comp—meaning she couldn't work for months and we'd go broke—she quickly came up with a plan, and, shit, it *worked*, too: Mom drove straight to her job at a high security mental hospital—imagine how painful that ride was!—concealed her injury when she punched in, summoned the hospital's most violent patient into a private room with her—a room that had no cameras—and then she told this madman, 'Listen, honey, I've noticed you making goo-goo eyes at me, so here's the deal—I'll suck you off if you pretend you went nuts today and stomped on me and broke my arm.'"

HAUNT ME OUT: A TRIPLE PLAY

"Let's grab a coffee when I'm back from vacation," I told my neighbor, a quiet white-haired academic who specialized in nineteenth-century medical textbooks, and he said, "Yes, with pleasure," but two weeks later when I stepped onto the landing that we shared, jetlagged and lugging a heavy suitcase, I found his apartment door covered with police tape and a notice listing his "Cause of Death" as "Homicide."

"We know who slashed his throat, it was a hustler who's fled back home to Bucharest, where we've been trying to track him down," explained the police (they'd left a letter on my door saying, "Call us"), and my relief on hearing this news was profound (so they knew knew who the culprit was and, better still, they knew it wasn't me!) but all that night and for a lot of nights thereafter, I felt too troubled to fall asleep, believing that those murderous vibrations were seeping now through our shared wall and flowing into my defenseless mind.

The French woman who moved into that apartment once the blood had been washed away had a formal air about her, and she seemed fearless—having heard about the murder, she said, "The past just doesn't scare me"—but after three months she for some reason went insane, smashing her windows, hurling garbage on folks below, blasting catchy Romanian pop songs on her turntable all night long, threatening our lives when we tried to reason with her, and barricading herself inside when the police at last showed up.

POWDER BLUE

Ben's mother once changed his diaper on the sink in a certain powder-blue-colored men's room at Newark Airport, and nineteen years later he had sex with a girlfriend in a stall in this same powder-blue room, and eight years after that he changed his own child's diaper on the sink in this powder-blue room, and forty-one years after that he died of a coronary while sitting on a toilet in this powder-blue room, but Ben never really noticed the room's recurring place in his life till that last moment when the whole place flooded with light which, for the record, was not colored powder-blue but magenta.

CRIME SOLVERS: HELSINKI

Someone stabbed to death a Roma man outside Map's cabin, so once the ship returned to port (they'd only set sail from Helsinki an hour earlier), the police chief came onboard, ordered everyone to the disco, and there he tried to solve the crime by walking up to every passenger (even children and the elderly), staring deeply into each face, then moving on or else declaring—as he did with fourteen people, including a very nervous Map—"Take this suspect away for questioning."

EL PRECIOSO MASTURBADOR

When we hit a mighty iceberg and our less-than-mighty ship went down, a blues singer sang a happy church hymn while a deist smashed his antique wristwatch and dumped the pieces overboard;

the ship's captain sought to cover up his negligence, fearing a painful bop from the karmic hammer;

an anarchist shot the ship's cook with a derringer, though he'd been aiming for the captain, while some soldiers onboard sang "Praise the Lord and Pass the Ammunition," with only a few of them out of tune;

a New Ageist plugged his asshole with a crystal;

a Utilitarian tried using the cook's corpse as a makeshift flotation device;

the ship's orchestra struck up "Hello Dolly" (having never learned to play "Nearer, My God, to Thee" and possessing no sheet music for it, anyway);

various businesspeople clashed over the right to buy the iceberg, tip and all;

a miniaturist painter frantically crammed her life's work into an empty bottle of Cold Duck;

an environmentalist blamed the ship for damaging the ocean while an anti-environmentalist cried, "You see? If global warming really existed, that iceberg would have already melted";

a rabbi, a priest, and an imam huddled together, thereby becoming fodder for a dumb joke mumbled by the anarchist;

a pleasure-seeker fucked the closest hole at hand, which was the nasty sucking chest wound in the cook's corpse;

some "normal" passengers entertained perverse notions while some perverts entertained more-perverse-than-usual notions;

one agnostic at last decided what was what while another remained "not sure just yet";

Joyce Carol Oates stayed in her cabin, calmly finishing her next book;

a dope enthusiast sang "Praise the Lord and Pass the Amyl Nitrite" as she rifled through her neighbors' medicine cabinets—

and all the while I stood on deck and watched the shit come rattling down, finally able to feel authentic—and masturbating like a fiend.

BUY YOURSELF SOME FREAK-OUT INSURANCE

During the Crisis, you took daily walks on the rural road near your new home, always making sure to wave your hand to greet your neighbors, including one who never waved back—he would just stand and glare at you—but when the Crisis critically worsened and he broke into your house with two armed men, he recognized you from those greetings you'd given him and so he left you with some food instead of stealing all of it.

How about a story about the "missing years" of Jesus, when some say he traveled to India but others say he found the path to Eden's west gate, where the angel posted there said, "Sorry, sir, no mortals allowed, your father's orders," and Jesus replied, "But I'm not mortal, only *half*, and my mortal half is bound to suffer and die in pain, so I prefer this peaceful spot, I want to stay in here forever," and feeling pity for God's son, the angel opened wide the gate and said, "In that case, be my guest," and yet instead of rushing in, Jesus hesitated, thinking, *When Papa learns I'm hiding here, he'll kick me out,* and so he switched the angel's body with his own, making them trade corporeal places, and now the angel, resembling Jesus, has started trudging toward the world, that awful place, while Jesus strokes his new left wing and thinks, *Of course I'd rather be* inside, *but standing watch here's still a better deal than what I had.*

108

GOING MAD TOGETHER

During her Classics seminar in college, Jules read a certain line from *Medea*, and even though she had no clue what it meant, she liked this line enough not to forget it during the three decades to come, decades she spent as a mostly unfulfilled wife and as a mostly fulfilled social worker, which is how she met the beautiful young homeless man whom she secretly took home with her and kept safe in a corner of her basement, where she fed him and whispered with him and made love with him each night when she went there to do the family laundry, and the morning when her husband came downstairs and found the young man and knocked him out with the tennis racket he'd gone to search for, Jules cradled her lover in her arms, looking up at Joe's enraged face, and didn't know what she should say except for that *Medea* line, which popped into her head as if it was waiting there for all those decades to get its cue: "*Old friend, I have to weep / The gods and I went mad together and we made things as they are.*"

A BUMBLEBEE ON YOM KIPPUR

It was Yom Kippur and I felt guilty, guilty not about skipping synagogue or eating lunch instead of fasting (I'd been a worse Jew before today), but guilty about hurting a bumblebee that was traipsing along the rim of my coffee cup when just for fun I knocked it into my French Roast, which really seemed to burn the thing, the coffee's acid scorching it like liquid fire, and after I fished the bee out and set it here on my café table, the poor thing thrashed around but then stopped, and I thought, *Damn, I've* killed *this creature, and on* Yom Kippur, *no less,* at which point the server, whose name was Gish (so said her name-tag), but who in fact was God herself, God herself in human form (she takes this form each Yom Kippur because it hones her judging skills), she gave that bee a close inspection, pronounced it dead (which sank my heart), shot me a disapproving look, said, "*Fail we may but sail we must*—this phrase is tattooed on many sailors," then breathed a few times on the bee, smiled when its wings moved, and turned to watch it sail away (with my restored heart like a stowaway on board).

BLOW ME DOWN

After the night we spent together, I woke up to find her gone, but she had scrawled two words in lipstick on my mirror, the words "*Murtis * Felatris*," which baffled me until I read a book on ancient Pompeii and learned of a sex worker there who wrote on a brothel wall the same words, which mean "Murtis the Blowjob Queen," right before Vesuvius erupted to bury her in ash but to preserve her sassy boast.

EVERYTHING TRIES TO BE ROUND

"Everything in life makes a circle, it's all about circles, circles within circles, because, like Black Elk said, everything is trying to be round"—so an Israeli woman told you once at a Hollywood garden party, and just as you were thinking, *She's barking mad*, you heard a buzzing sound above you and looked up to find a skywriting plane forming the third *O* in "USE COLGATE TOOTHPASTE," at which point something clicked, and from then on you kept seeing circles, nothing but circles, circles within circles, and your favorite one of them was in a tale about Cavafy, the great Greek modernist poet, who lay dying in his home, surrounded by friends, when he asked for pen and paper (*His final poem,* thought everyone, delighted), and now they watched as he gripped the pen with his feeble hand, drew a circle on the paper, put a dot at the circle's center, then dropped the pen, eased back his body, and surrendered to any circles yet to come.

THE WALL UP

Our housekeeper Frau Schmeding—Elisabeth Schmeding of the Black Forest—was like a second mother to us, and we loved to hear her stories:

how her boss, an anti-Nazi lawyer, was dictating a letter when the Gestapo hauled him away and then rang his wife a few days later to tell her where to claim his corpse;

how Frau Schmeding, now working as a cook at a mountain inn where Hitler came to dine once, peeked through the kitchen doors at the teetotal vegetarian *fürher* who sat rail-straight while his officers feasted on boar and drunkenly passed out around him;

how the good Frau's parents and first husband and first child were all killed in Allied bombing raids and yet she chose to come live in America, anyway;

and we remember, too, her little dachshund, and her love for Schweppes Ginger Ale, and the false teeth in the glass on her bathroom sink, and how she'd shout, "You drive me the wall *up*" whenever we, such terrible children, teamed up to annoy her.

WHATEVER SHE BRINGS, WE SING

"A brain tumor," declared not one but two different specialists in Brussels, "you've only got a few months to live," so Lyle flew home to his family in Baltimore, where his cousin, a neurosurgeon, said, "Let me examine you myself," and sure enough, this cousin found that Lyle's tumor was not a tumor, after all, but an aneurysm, something the cousin was able to cure with an emergency operation, and later when Lyle said, "So I guess I'm a lucky man," his cousin agreed, saying, "Luckier than you know, because when you took that recent flight from Brussels with your not-yet-diagnosed aneurysm, well, you didn't realize this, of course, but you had a ninety-nine percent chance of dying from the air pressure in that plane."

OUT, DEMONS, OUT!

Fearing that one of my fellow guests at the wedding reception would stumble over the large brick that lay on the churchyard lawn, I leaned down to move it, but as soon as I did, I realized my mistake: the brick had been placed there to cover a small hole, and it was not just any hole that someone might step into but a hole out of which dozens of hornets now flew, furious perhaps at having been trapped underground and intent on wreaking vengeance on us (oddly, the bride and groom suffered the most stings), and as I watched this chaos I'd caused, all the shouting and the running to-and-fro, I said to myself, *As usual, son, you meant well, but as usual, son, you fucked it all up.*

WAKE UP, YOU

Ever since you read about the Hindu *Vasudeva*—"the best and highest of all people, of whom only one is living at any given moment"—you've been seeking him or her, wondering, *Could it be this wise young girl? This gentle old man? This laughing baby?*, unaware that the *Vasudeva* was in fact the maid at a Memphis motel who knocked on your door too early one morning and who heard you yelling at her from your lumpy bed, *"Go away, you motherfucker, I'm still asleep!"*

ROCK 'N' ROLL HERNIA (2)

"Who *are* you?" the talk-show host asks Benny Pompa, but the Kabbalah-savvy rock star says nothing, he merely stares back at the host in silence for a full minute until he finally nods his head and whispers, "I just answered your question but you weren't listening."

EIGHT LADIES FROM THE LATE EIGHTIES

When the senility began to crowd out all the memories from Brent's mind, he fought back by leaving notes around his house in random spots, notes which bore the names of all his lovers when he was single:

"Pansy Sapp" (she hadn't understood why people found her name amusing);

"Julie Lippman" (an Englishwoman Brent had met on the Côte d'Azur);

"Samantha Juarez" (she'd denied being Hispanic and brutally beat up a male law school classmate of hers who claimed she was);

"Penny Martis" (a secretary who catapulted through the ranks of a local political campaign to end up serving as chief-of-staff for a national presidential candidate);

"Malaika Tshishekedi" (the daughter of Zembla's ambassador to Switzerland, this ambassador serving—it only occurred to Brent much later—as the "bagman" for a most corrupt dictatorship);

"Gina Taddler" (a medical student who got sand in Brent's bed after they swam naked in Lake Michigan and whose boyfriend, another med student, found out about Brent and threatened his life);

"Vulterine" (a Goth Turkish hairstylist for whose attention Brent drunkenly ran into a plate-glass wall, after which he wound up in the local ER where the intern assigned to put stitches in his eyebrow turned out to be that same med student who'd threatened Brent's life because of Gina Taddler);

"Emma Jonas" (a baker who informed Brent only after they slept together on her sofa while music by Soul Asylum played over and over that she was HIV-positive)—

—and soon it reached the point where Brent would find these notes around his house yet fail to recognize the names on them ("Pansy Sapp? Who's Pansy Sapp? And Emma Jonas…?") so he would dream up new memories to go with each ("Ah, yes, I met Pansy in that tavern on Lemuria before it sank into the sea, and as for this Emma, well, when I was struggling up Fern Hill on my unicycle, she loaned me her go-cart"), and even though Brent's senility fought hard against these new scenes, these wild inventions, that senility kept getting thwarted, because imagination now had the upper hand.

WHO PUT THE BENZEDRINE IN GARY LIPPMAN'S OVALTINE?

The porn actress at the Tribeca dinner party showed me a video on her phone, a video of herself caressing a dozen naked sex dolls hung on meathooks, and every doll was fabricated to look and feel exactly like herself, which reminded me of my birthday party when I turned fifty and all my younger selves showed up—all the forty-nine younger Garys, a Gary Lippman for every year— and the only ones I could bear to spend any time with were the children, because the rest of those guys, each so familiar, just made me see how little I've changed since puberty.

ANOTHER VERSION OF AHASUERUS

Among the multitudes who've gathered in shocked silence near Notre Dame to watch it burn through the night, only one pair of eyes has also looked on the four churches that preceded the cathedral here, as well as the Roman temple on this spot *before* those churches—eyes that belong to Ahasuerus, the "Wandering Jew," a man condemned by Jesus to walk the earth till Judgment Day—and never, in all the centuries he's wandered, has he forgotten the gold-flecked eyes of a priestess he'd met at that Roman temple, eyes he believes he can see now in the flames that whip the darkness with their light.

ULTIMA THULE, DO YER STUFF!

As soon as I stepped into the bathroom in that wine bar on MacDougal Street, the odor of the soap they used to clean the toilet hit my nose like a bazooka shell, because it was the same soap, Ultima Thule, that my parents cleaned our own toilet with when I was young, young and happy, and because I hadn't smelled this fragrance since then, the power of the memory, this paradise regained, nailed me to that spot, my nostrils sucking in the soap-scent, and my dead father was with me now, and my dead mother was with me, too, and we forgave each other everything as I ignored you customers who started knocking on the door ("We need to use it!"), and I ignored the wine bar's owner ("I'll call the cops!"), and I ignored the gruff policeman who finally showed up—I just remained there in the bathroom, basking in that sentimental medicine, and when the cop yelled, "You can't stay in there forever!" (right before he broke down the door), I spoke at last, informing him, and all of you, and this entire break-doors-down world, "*Oh yes I can.*"

A CLOWN ISN'T FUNNY IN THE MOONLIGHT

Tangled black hair, a crazy smile, and leaning toward me for some reason: I took a snapshot of this girl on a Dublin road and, since she looked so otherworldly, I put it online with the mischievous caption *"She wasn't there when I shot this photo, so could this be a ghost?"* which fooled nobody, of course, but today in a museum far from Dublin, here she is again, the same girl only now she's in a painting, a painting from a century ago, a painting entitled *Happy Frolics*, and as she leans out from the canvas and I lean away, disturbed, her crazy smile seems to ask, "Who's fooling who?"

THIS STORYTELLER'S BEGINNING

Whenever the child followed his mother's orders—pouring hot sauce on his father's food, using scissors to cut up his stepmother's clothing, falsely telling the judge in the endless custody battle, "My dad mistreats me"—his father spanked him but his mother bought him toys, so the child quickly learned not to follow his mother's orders but to tell her that he did, which meant no spankings, lots of those toys, and expert training as a liar.

TOO MUCH PORK FOR JUST ONE FORK

"Praise the Lord and pass the amyl nitrite—here at The Groove Farm we've got both hands on the thunderbolt machine, with drastic measures for mindless pleasures, and hearts on stilts who glance and gulp, decking your bosoms with dinner bells, drinking gasoline spo-dee-o-dee and asking, 'Why must you call me "Snuffy"? while you adjust your vibrating jowl strap—oh, yes, folks, it's here at The Groove Farm, where we're overweight but still not over you—how could we be? how could we ever?— we, who got toilet-trained in tiger pits, and melted down in vats of weltschmerz, not to mention wang-dang-doodle (that old one-two punch!), while all the while we tried to live up to our baby pictures, yes, crying, "Kiss me, I'm confused," yes, trimming our thongs with a blowtorch, yes, right when the moon slides underwater and the stars steal up your spine and then to hell on a hang-glider we will go" —*

at which point the carnie barker paused to cough and a young girl in the crowd who'd been savoring his words looked at her father and told him, beaming, "Screw being a nurse when I grow up—*this* is what I wanna do!"

LULU LORE: A TRIPLE PLAY

The Jews say, "Those in a hurry do not arrive," the Muslims say, "If you're in a hurry, you're already dead," and then there was the hundred-year-old Grandma Lulu, who I assumed would relish hearing about the latest high-tech breakthroughs, so one day I read to her of how future airplanes would utilize rockets to boost their speed and fly from New York to Beijing in just an hour, but instead of *ooh*'ing and *aah*'ing at this news, Lulu looked sad, almost as though she pitied me, and with a shrug of her shoulders she said, "What's the hurry?"

~~~~~~

At one-hundred-and-one, Grandma Lulu said, "There's a younger man I know who wants to date me," and so, fearing a gigolo, I said, "How *much* younger?" and Lulu said, "He's ninety," so I laughed and said, "Well, why *don't* you date him?" and Lulu said, "Oh, no, I'm still faithful to your grandfather's memory"—but then she added, "That doesn't mean, though, that I don't still get my *urges*."

~~~~~~

About that grandfather: "Sometimes when I'm ill," Lulu said, "I see him standing across the room and I call out, 'Please, Davey, help me,' but he looks so sad when he says, 'I'm sorry, Lu, I'm just too far away'"—and the morning Lulu died, her doctor told me, "She was alone in her room when it happened but right before that I heard her speaking as if someone was there with her," so I thought, *Maybe this time Davey was able to get close enough.*

"Stop," my stomach shouts, "this can't go on, there's no more room, you'll overload me," but my brain says, "That's too bad, because I've eaten most of this quadruple-sized hamburger already, and the deal at the restaurant here is, if I finish the whole thing, I don't have to pay for it," so my stomach says, "You were warned," and it erupts, after which my brain goes into shame mode and the angry busboy with the mop says, "Almost *every fucking customer*."

KICK

Pryna's had her share of one night stands that ended strangely, but only one that *started* strangely—the one in Reno where the card dealer she'd just met frowned at the locked front door of his bungalow and said, "God dammit, I lost my keys again, but, well, your cowboy boots look sturdier than mine, so would you please kick in my door?" and even though Pryna at first thought, *Am I on* Candid Camera?, she was just drunk enough, and just horny enough, to soon be tearing the dealer's shirt off while his front door hung grotesquely from one hinge.

PRETTY MUCH NOT YOUR STANDARD
SADDLE SORE

"When a pal of mine, a federal judge, died of a stroke while 'in the saddle' with a hooker at a motel, the hooker fled but the judge's take-charge clerk, who'd been waiting outside, called three of the judge's colleagues for help, so they drove there, helped the clerk dress the corpse in its three-piece suit, wrapped it up in a Persian carpet they'd brought with them, loaded the corpse into a car, and drove it to the courthouse, where the clerk told the night watchman they were dropping off the rug, then propped the corpse up at its desk and rang the judge's wife to say, 'We just came in and found him like this'—and after my father recounted this story to me, I said, "So you were one of those guys who helped the clerk, right?"

DRESS SEXY AT MY FUNERAL

I used to want my epitaph to read "NO STONE UNTURNED, EXCEPT FOR THIS ONE," but lately I prefer a sentence found by New York City's fireworks commissioner when he climbed to the Brooklyn Bridge's highest point one night and noticed there a graffito scrawled on a parapet, a graffito which will, I submit to you, look just *perfect* on my tombstone: "YOU'VE COME A LONG WAY, BABY, NOW LET'S SEE HOW FAR YOU CAN FLY."

NUTS FOR MAUGHAM

"What inspired you to become a writer?" I asked Brock, a successful tough-guy novelist who'd spent thirty years in Sing Sing for armed robbery, and Brock's reply was, "It was Maugham, Somerset Maugham, I loved his books, I'm nuts for Maugham," which amused me (just picture this hardened convict reading that old-fashioned English author in a prison library!) until I recalled the rumor that Maugham sold his soul to Satan in exchange for literary fame, which got me wondering whether Brock had done the same thing.

O, WHAT A BLOODY MANICHEAN MESS...

Of the many mistakes I made that day, my first was to jump over the subway turnstile, trying to beat the fare;

my second mistake was to argue with the police officer who busted me and began to write me a ticket;

my third mistake was to get visibly annoyed by the scary-looking thug who'd walked up to mock me, saying, "You little pussy, getting caught for turnstile-hopping";

my fourth mistake was to feel so protected by the cop's presence that I dared to shout, "Fuck you" at the thug;

my fifth mistake was to fail to conceal my fear when the thug grew furious and said, "Oh, now we got *business*—as soon as this cop splits, I'm gonna *crush* you";

my sixth mistake was to assume I'd get some protection from the cop once I said, "Did you hear that, officer? This man just threatened me";

but the cop just chortled and said, "That's *your* business, not mine—as soon as I give you your ticket, you two can settle this beef yourselves";

and so I decided to stop making mistakes, telling myself, *Now that I've gotten on the wrong side of both cop and thug, law and disorder, all I can do is take my ticket, then take my beating, and then, if I survive, drag myself home and climb in bed and never leave that bed again.*

CATCH

I remember my mother playing catch with me in our backyard because I didn't have a father at home to do it; and I remember that when the softball struck her left tit once, causing her to wince in pain, she said, "This is how women get breast cancer"; and now, fifty years on, I'm watching a different mother and different son play catch in Golden Gate Park, and I'm thinking of the woman *I* played catch with (guess what kind of cancer killed her?), and I'm thinking, *Sure, we need you, fathers—but we get by just fine without you.*

CHATTY

"No one believes I'm Jewish," said the chatty Ethiopian realtor as she led me through the apartment that she deemed "deliciously right" for me ("The shower even fits seven people," she strangely boasted), "but I was raised in Tel Aviv, although we went a lot to South America because my father, a big economist, would get sent there to counsel governments, and he also had a side job, which was spotting local Nazis, all the elderly Nazi fugitives hiding out there since the war, and once he'd find them, he'd call his boss at the Mossad, who'd send an assassination team."

IF THE WORLD WAS PERFECT, IT WOULDN'T BE

Pryna told her father, "I know how much you admire Yogi Berra, Dad, so when I met him at a charity event last night, I asked him to sign a baseball for you, and he wrote, '*Hey pal, too bad we never got to meet*,'" which made her father chuckle and say, "Actually, I *did* hang out with Yogi once, on a golf course when you were three, and when I asked him to sign a baseball for you, he wrote, '*Hey, Pryna, I hope we'll get to meet someday*.'"

BU LOI

Having learned about her fifty-three years of being overworked, neglected, physically abused, and raped repeatedly (although her keepers merely called these rapes "forced breeding"), my wife and I would visit Bu Loi in her enclosure each day after finishing our work at the Thai elephant sanctuary, both of us cooing to her and petting her curved hard forehead when she extended it to us and basically just honoring this fellow creature for how she'd endured so much pain with such grace, a grace that too few of the people Bu Loi encountered had ever bothered to show to her.

LADIES AND GENTLEMEN, AUNT MINNIE!

Ever since she left her far-off village, the married woman living in Seoul has heard from fortune tellers, "But you're a *widow*, the stars say so!" and whenever she hears this she merely smiles at her husband, who's unaware that at nineteen she'd loved a boy who was a pilot and whose plane crashed only one month after their wedding and so, worried that no one would marry a widow, young or not, her parents moved the family to Seoul and then behaved as if that first marriage never happened.

CHRISTMAS ON EARTH EVERY DAY

How sad, Pryna thought as the one-armed young man walked past her table at the outdoor café in Antwerp, *I wonder how he lost his arm,* but then he moved his shoulder in such a way that, *presto,* the missing limb appeared in view—he'd just been reaching behind himself to scratch his back, so the missing limb was an illusion, just a trick of the summer light, and Pryna felt happy for the man, thinking, *Yes, you're complete,* and for a moment other miracles seemed possible: people would appreciate their having two arms, and wrongs both great and small would be made right, and the dead would rise, feeling fiddle-fit, and we'd inhabit (no exceptions!) the "Christmas on earth every day" that Rimbaud spoke of.

WATCH US VANISH

"You haunted each other": this phrase from a Thomas Pynchon novel has gotten you imagining two ghosts—bitter rivals during life and neither one now yet aware that her foe is also dead—and these ghosts scare one another with every trick in the haunting handbook, making their afterlives a misery when they could yield to fate instead and simply float around in peace till Judgment Day.

DOG IN FOG

V. and I fell in love dancing to swing band music in a Krakow bar called "Dog In Fog" (according to the motto on the front door, "It Will Always Find Its Way Home"), but the roof was so low that we sometimes bumped our heads, and a drunk man kept interrupting us to say he'd lost his EpiPen ("My allergies is can to be fatal," he'd informed us in warped English), so we helped him search for that EpiPen on the grimy floor but couldn't find it—"Sorry," we finally said—and just before we left that place, I accidentally dropped my glass of beer, which didn't shatter but rolled beneath our table, and when V. leaned down to grab it she discovered something else, a certain object, but the owner of this object had left the Dog In Fog by then and so we dashed into the street, which was thick with revelers (have I mentioned it was New Year's Eve?), and because V. and I had just fallen in love, and new love works like magic, we soon caught sight of someone in that crowd, a lonely figure weaving drunkenly along, and together we ran after him, shouting in a single joyous voice, "Hey, man, we *found* it!"

SMASHED FULL OF WONDER

I was writing in my journal when I heard your voice outside, but you were speaking in a girl's voice, not the woman's voice I've known, so I went to watch you mingle with your school friends, playing hopscotch, and when I finally came back in I found that I'd been gone for decades, and everyone I knew was dead, including you, whose child-voice was so bewitching.

ONE BABY TO ANOTHER SAYS...

"Maybe you should calm her down," I told the young blond stoned American stranger outside the Nirvana concert in Stockholm in '92, "her" being his pregnant girlfriend who kept shrieking at a T-shirt vendor, "Give us some *free merch*, you fucking asshole," but the stranger just mumbled to me, "She's cool, man, it's cool, man," and I'd almost forgotten him once Nirvana took the stage and I saw he was the singer.

I'M FOREVER BLOWING BUBBLES

Last month, not a day passed in which you didn't hear somebody use the word "bubble," and this phenomenon seemed too bizarre to be coincidental: Were the Fates reminding you that you'd been living in a bubble of good fortune, a bubble about to pop, *or* should you fear a death by drowning, your mouth emitting bubbles as you sink, *or*—looking on the bright side for a change—would you order bubble tea at that new café on Goshen Crescent and find inside it a bubble-like rare pearl, one so priceless that you won't mind breaking a few teeth when you chomp down hard on it?

THE WHAMMY, AZTEC STYLE

The moment they stole that magic stone orb from the mad-eyed Aztec priest (blood was matted in his hair even before they hacked him up), the two conquistadors got whooshed into the future—the battlefield at Gettysburg, to be exact, right in the middle of rabid fighting—and they cut down seven Grays and thirteen Blues before a SWAT team took them out, because they *hadn't* wound up in combat, after all, but rather smack dab in the middle of what we call a "movie set."

SHORTIES: A SMORGASBORD WITH ZOMBIE BUTTER

I'd always been a fan of the adage "If you sit by the river long enough, you'll see the body of your enemy go floating past you" until the day my daughter and I were fishing at a bend of the Danube and the bloated corpse of her beloved pediatrician splashed around a bend and then rolled straight toward us.

꙳꙳꙳

Jesus came back, undetected by anyone except for a Maori girl named Lili; he took a fairly good look around; and then he contacted his father on his quantum walkie-talkie and said, "Pops, let's just start over."

꙳꙳꙳

The loudest conversation I ever heard came from a dozen kids near the Boul Mich one summer evening who "spoke" to one another, deaf as they were, using nothing but their hands.

꙳꙳꙳

When Map crashed his first Jewish singles mixer while wearing his "EVERYBODY LOVES A *YIDDISHE* BOY" t-shirt, no one spoke to him, so for the next mixer he wore a sweater that read, "EVEN HITLER HAD A GIRLFRIEND—WHY CAN'T I?" and that night he got three phone numbers, a French kiss, plus a rather smoldering slow dance.

∿∿∿

Troy was a junkie, the only child of a Bel Air gynecologist, and when we went together once to an LA art museum, he especially liked a Renaissance-era *Crucifixion*, gazing at the canvas for a long spell before he turned to me and said, "The painter must've bribed those Roman soldiers to let him stand so close to the cross."

∿∿∿

132   "But if you *don't* learn to wipe your dirty tushy," Pryna told her toddler, "who's gonna do it when you're older and Mommy's not there to help?" and the boy, very much his father's child, just made a sour face at Pryna (oh, how *foolish* Mommy was!) and then informed her, "My wife, who else?"

∿∿∿

It was a bad night at Pukersdorf when that asylum's new head doctor foolishly lodged a man with Klüver-Bucy Syndrome, in which the victim felt the nonstop urge to eat and fuck, in the same room as a man with Cotard Delusion, in which the victim felt utterly convinced that he was dead.

∿∿∿

When we walked by an Arab woman with cobalt-blue eyes in Old Jerusalem, my uncle Wolf theorized, "Crusader genes," but some years later on a pueblo near Mesa Grande, we met a Kumeyaay elder who said his name was "Rabinowitz," and when I glanced at my uncle, Wolf just shrugged and whispered, "Your guess is as good as mine."

At a bookstore, you told your friend, "What a bummer I won't live long enough to read everything I want," but Jon, refusing to find scarcity in this abundance, said, "Me, I'm *glad* there's too many books, because I know I'll never run out."

This too-sharp-for-his-own-good country bumpkin, he refused to loan you money—you, the dissipated rogue with a taste for language and learning—but once you're gone, Greene, that bumpkin will do right by you, after all, by resurrecting you and knighting you and granting you a new name: "Falstaff."

"Are you hungry?" you heard the waitress ask the smiling old man at the table beside yours, and "Sure am," he said, though his smile dimmed a bit when he added, "and what I want for dinner is a trout my father caught in Lake Huron in the summer of '63."

While sitting at a bar and stroking the long-haired head of her new lover, Pryna suddenly recoiled because the top of the guy's skull felt like it came to a point, yet instead of getting miffed by her reaction, the guy just laughed and said, "Pinheads *do* exist, we're not just in freak shows, and I'm the cutest one you'll meet."

When the creepy children's fiction author signed his new book to my young son with the words "*To a Future Orphan*," I told the man, "Isn't that a little morbid?" but he was ready for my complaint and snapped at me, "Surely you don't want to *outlive* your child?"

Finally fed up with the Japanese tour guide who'd nearly blinded her by surrounding her each day with hordes of flashbulb-flashing clients, the old elephant could still see well enough to seize that tour guide with her trunk, pin him to the pavement, and use her right foot to stomp him flat.

When I inquired about the big scar near her eye, the woman at the party said, "My brother hit me with his book-bag when I was six," so I said, "Why don't you make up a more dramatic story?", and later on, sure enough, I heard her tell some Lebanese guy, "I climbed a tree once and found a nest and reached for it— 'Here, little birdies'—then out of nowhere some eagle soared down and tried to tear my goddamned *eye* out."

What are the odds that each time Map opens the *I Ching* and throws the yarrow sticks, the hexagram he receives, even well into his old age, is always "*Youthful Folly*"?

Try though they sometimes did, no one who lived or worked at the nursing home could understand what the senile old amputee kept muttering to himself—no one but the gods, who hardly cared: "I miss my leg."

ᴀᴡᴡᴡ

Over Mint Juleps we sat complaining about the government until this Austrian journalist named Karl Kraus approached us and said, "If you actually perceived the true reality behind the news, you'd all run screaming into the street, so just enjoy your cocktails, boys—and buy me one, too, while you're at it?"

ᴀᴡᴡᴡ

Last night Map and his friends jumped in a boiling sea of breasts, breasts of different shapes and sizes—with some of us doing cannonballs, others swan dives or belly flops—but of everyone who surfaced (a few did not), Map was the only man who came up sucking not a nipple but his own thumb.

ᴀᴡᴡᴡ

"I can't seem to get this IV to stick into your wrist," the nurse says, jabbing your forearm with a hypodermic needle for a third time, and then, as if you aren't already scared enough about your surgery tomorrow, a male voice from beyond the curtain to your left says, "*I* can do it if you want—I'm a mortician."

ᴀᴡᴡᴡ

I'd just arrived at St. Eve's party when a reveler began to vomit blood and then collapsed and didn't move, but for some reason no one seemed to care (one guy even laughed at how freaked-out I'd gotten), and I was calling 911 when St. Eve took my phone and calmly explained what everyone else already knew: "He just drank too much cherry-colored alcoholic fruit punch."

W. S. Merwin wrote a poem about how, every year, we live through the day on which we'll eventually die, never aware of that day's future significance (for Merwin, it was the fifteenth of March), but think of how much else about our deaths we unknowingly miss—like that elm tree you drive past every day, that elm tree patiently waiting for you to crash into it.

~~~~~~

Hank Williams and my father were born on the same day in the same year, and even though they never met and they died sixty years apart, my father says, "Hank and I both ripped off Jack Ruby—Hank never showed up for a gig at Ruby's Dallas nightclub and I never paid a gambling debt I owed Jack—so I guess we lucked out that Ruby shot Oswald, not me or Hank."

While you strolled together through the Luxembourg Gardens one summer evening, your eight-year-old watched all the smoking, drinking, laughing, singing teenagers and he thought, *Someday I'll be just like them* even as you eyed the same kids and thought of how you'd once been just like them but wish you'd enjoyed the experience more.

Back when he was a young tailor in Budapest, Pryna's great-grandfather used to stand beside a sphinx statue outside the opera house on opening nights in order to check out the audience members' latest fashions, a fact he once told Pryna but which she'd forgotten by the time she and a drummer who was staying at her hotel kissed behind that same sphinx a century later.

"This asshole from Poland said that Warsaw's just like San Francisco but without the fucking faggots," Map told the gay man from Cleveland he'd just befriended, "so I said, 'Listen, you fucking homophobe, I've heard that you Poles were worse than Nazis in World War II and now I *believe* it"—at which point Map's new friend said, "I'm Polish-American and I resent that, you fucking xenophobe."

After Sandy began work as a doorman in our building, we noticed we weren't getting all our mail, and then one night on TV we saw that Sandy, while getting busted for mail fraud, had fled into our building's basement, where he kept the police at bay with a shotgun while screaming his ex-wife's name, and now that Sandy's out of prison, he's been living in his car outside our building and asking us if we can possibly forgive him.

As they streaked through the Void toward whatever fate would greet them, one newly perished soul said of his life, "First I was raw, then I was cooked" but another soul scoffed at this and said, "*Me*, I burned, I burned, I burned."

TRAPDOOR TO HADES

While I'm unable to summarize in one sentence my friend Thornton Pisher's new novel *The Neon Suburb* (and trust me, I've tried), I'll at least mention some of the characters, who include the hero Hannibal Bell, Cappy Montdekka (Bell's actuary sidekick), Fra Filippo Lipschitz (unkind nightclub owner), Froma Rose (Lipschitz's actuary mistress), Jervis Mignon (tart-tongued cop), Ted Shelightner (castrated corpse found on page 26), S. F. Donahoo (Shelightner's cross-dressing, and double-crossing, chess instructor), Nefertiti Bako (one-legged cigarette girl), Ephraim A La Carte (child prodigy gun runner), "Light and Salty" (a chanteuse specializing in Jimmy Webb songs), Trixie Alpha-Mix (Classics scholar "with a past"), Dwight S. Hih (Chinese nasal-spray-addicted physician), Billy Dry Socket (Lakota bounty hunter), and Veronica Lustig (the castrating murderer, who's based entirely on the author's mother).

ME AND MY MEDUSA

The night Jim Morrison died, I was a frightened kid sleeping for the first time in my father's new house where, taped to a bedroom wall, was my new stepbrother's poster in which the Doors singer's long hair looked like snakes, cruel snakes my dad had set loose on my life, and all night long I stayed awake lest those snakes or my new family murder me, although years later, having come to love Jim's music, I stole that poster and might still have it tucked away somewhere.

CUPID: THE MOTHERFUCKER

That's the boy I'm gonna marry, Pryna thought when she first beheld the purple-t-shirt-wearing Guy Oonen in her fifth-grade class, but Guy never went near her, much less glanced in her direction, until the middle of one science lab when he jumped up abruptly and ran straight toward Pryna, his arms opened wide, and so she thought, *Wow, he* does *love me, after all*, not realizing that this boy hurried not to her but to the bathroom door behind her, and since he didn't make it in time, he wound up vomiting on Pryna's desk.

ONCE A FATHER, ONCE A SON

Marching past me at Miami Airport were a man and his eight- or nine-year-old son, both of them clad in three-piece suits, with the boy looking like a small version of the man, their arms swinging in sync as they walked (perhaps to meet a just-landed relative), and being a father and a son myself, I turned to watch them for a moment, smiling at the boy's adult-like movements while waiting for, hoping for, a certain gesture, and—*yes*, there it was, just before they vanished from view: the son's right arm stopped swinging and his hand reached to grasp his father's.

TERRI MAE HAD BAD LUCK WITH SAMOYEDS

Terri Mae had bad luck with Samoyeds: first our puppy Deaner ate some rat poison the previous owner left in our basement (I ran a lot of red lights to reach the vet but too late, too late), and then Terri told me how when she was ten she'd watched Trike, her puppy of the same breed, get murdered by a shotgun-wielding neighbor in Alabama (she'd tried to catch Trike as he ran onto that neighbor's lawn but too late, too late), and Terri only stopped crying a few days afterward when a trio of masked men (coincidentally, she had three violent teenage brothers) jumped the puppy-killer outside a bar and broke his four limbs and the local sheriff, who understood all, never raised a finger to find the culprits.

THE SPY WHO LIKED TO MIX RED WINE WITH COCA-COLA

The following sentence appears in the coded journal of a British intelligence officer (MI6) who was found dead in Brighton in 1984 under suspicious circumstances: "*I wonder what's become of Josefina Schultz, the German double agent who I worked with in East Berlin three years back and who seduced the Dutch ambassador and then blackmailed him into smuggling her to freedom through Checkpoint Charlie via a hiding space beneath a seat in his limousine, after which Josefina vanished and the ambassador, that naïve fool, was found dead in the Hague under 'suspicious circumstances.'*"

SHOCKER

Sweet Pea was a Spandex-clad rock groupie in eighties Hollywood who was already sleeping with two lead singers when she began to sleep with Map—"I like to shock you innocent college boys," she explained—and at the time she bought her hard drugs from a licensed pharmacist named Sal who'd once killed a larcenous friend of Pea's by injecting air bubbles into the thief's veins, but after awhile Pea forgave Sal, and one night she got so fucked up that she stole from Sal herself and pinned the blame on Map, which certainly shocked that "college boy," but after awhile Map and Sal both forgave Pea, so everything was cool again, and they went on partying at the Rainbow and the Central and Barney's Beanery and at an art gallery that only showed paintings of Kojak, partying together till Pea found work as a mud wrestler and then got strung out and disappeared, so Map went searching for her but couldn't find her ("Our pretty bird just flew away," said Sal), and now Map smiles when he recalls the very first night he spent with Pea and how she secretly took a big chomp from a hamburger before she kissed him, shocking Map with all the hot meat, ketchup, mustard, relish, and onions that filled his mouth along with Pea's delicious tongue.

IN ESTHER THERE IS NO EAST OR WEST

The tattoo on Gersh's arm is of a brown two-headed cow with its larger head X'ed out and the words "I SURVIVED ESTHER LIMSKY" beneath the hooves, this tattoo referencing the autumn day when Gersh was six and his mother Esther brought him to a state fair where they encountered just such a creature, and as he gawked at it, afraid to touch it, feeling awe and terror both at once, Esther said, "Look, dear, it's *us*, Gersh and Mommy, two heads together on one strong body, because you're the love of Mommy's life—my little man, my *only* man—so we can't live without each other, I'd die without you, you'd die without me, it's the two of us against the world, *just like this cow.*"

MOVING MERCURY AROUND

In case you're curious, here's what happened in New York City at 10:47 a.m. on the eighth of December, 1980:

a public-school janitor, aged fifty-six, wept in his supply room while reading a book entitled *Honest Abe: A Biography for Children*;

"For years," a woman, seventy-eight, told a pharmacist, "what's pulled me through my bad patches is a record of Armenian flute songs—and it hasn't been the music that's helpful, but just the *title* of the record, which is *I Will Not Be Sad in This World*";

after picking three pockets dry, a man, forty-two, was hurrying toward a city bus's rear door when he spotted Gaines, that plainclothes asshole, waiting to get on board, so the pickpocket had no choice but to reverse course and put each wallet back where it belonged;

high on the stupefying street drug called "Plotz" (whose side effect could make non-Yiddish speakers able to speak Yiddish), a woman, twenty-seven, was jogging through Central Park when she came upon a wounded red-tailed hawk and realized that, high or not, she would have to somehow kill this creature to end its pain;

a Frenchman, eighty-five, lay in bed remembering the Flanders trench he and his frightened comrades occupied one spring day in 1916, and how a family of rats had licked the brilliantine off the soldiers' hair;

a woman, sixty-nine, who was visiting the States for the first time, discovered that the American dollars she'd received from the bank in her Finnish village were not valid—in fact, they were Confederate currency—a situation she would have laughed about were she not now penniless and far from home;

a man, twenty-six, remembered while at his boring desk job how an elderly woman seated beside him at a recent performance of *Titus Andronicus* fainted and toppled over with her warm face in his lap, which led the whole theater, actors included, to stare at them in silence until some rogue from two rows over shouted, "Look, she's *blowing* him!";

a woman, thirty-six, began to love her child as a *person*, not just as her kin, when they walked past a homeless man who clutched a cardboard sign that read, "I'm hungry," and the girl, forgetting her initial fear of the man, ran to him and gave him her day's supply of candy;

a woman, fifty-one, who was a grief counselor by trade, was a long time dying in a hospice till death finally overtook her and she whispered to herself (it was her life's greatest surprise), "Wow, here it *comes*, it's actually happening to *me*";

while seated on a toilet in her new boyfriend's condo and discovering too late a lack of toilet paper there, a woman, thirty-two, yelled to her boyfriend's child, "Hon, where does Daddy keep the toilet paper?" and the girl yelled back, "In the bathroom, you imbecile, where *else*?"

three nude sloe-eyed beauties coiled themselves around the torso of a man, forty, as his child ran toward him, leaped in the air, and scored a direct hit by landing with her right knee in the man's groin right before the erotic dream he was having in his bed could reach its climax;

"Dust is composed of dead human skin cells," a scholar, sixty-three, told his lover, which the lover would remember twelve years later when he used a fingertip to write the words "YOU TAUGHT ME SO MUCH" in the dust of his now-gone beloved's bookshelf;

a woman, thirty-one, gazed at a street sign that read "Avenue of the Strongest," trying to figure out what it meant (just who *were* these "Strongest" people and why was a part of the city named for them?), this woman not suspecting that nine years later she would get married on this street;

a woman, forty-seven, who worked as a medical examiner, cut open up the victim of an airplane crash (the corpse half-eaten by shrimp before they pulled it from the sea) and, lo and behold, she found shrimp *inside* the victim, too—half-digested shrimp cocktail from the in-flight meal's first course;

a couple, fifty-five and thirty-nine, discussed while eating breakfast their recent journey to Tulum, where they floated down a river wearing life-preservers like diapers, feeling more blissful than they'd ever felt together, oblivious to the alligators who watched their progress from the riverbank;

a man, sixty-seven, who was a lifelong committer of violent crimes, lay very ill (he would eventually recover) and amazed his daughter when he mumbled, "May God forgive me, at ten years old I stole some money from my father, I can't *believe* it, I stole from *him,* from my own *father*...";

"Do you have the book *The Stranger* by Albert Camus?" a girl, twelve, asked her school librarian, proud of her desire to read something intellectual but mispronouncing the name as "*Came-uss,*" and the librarian put her in her place by saying, "Young lady, that author is *Spanish,* so the correct pronunciation of his name is '*Com-oose*'";

in the same library, a boy, also twelve, swiped a copy of *Emily Post's Guide to Etiquette* (which, in case you're curious, remains this nation's second-most-stolen book after the Bible);

a woman, fifty-one, told her ex-girlfriend when she bumped into her at Penn Station, "I've had three children since we broke up, but I still love our dream-child the most";

three male roommates, all twenty-six, had sex together while their favorite song to have sex to, Pearl Bailey singing "Seventy-Six Trombones," blared from their stereo; a woman, forty-five, laughed at the water cooler in an office when her boss, seventy-three, used a slang phrase while referring to a friend who'd just died, saying that the recently departed had "caught a cab";

"A new street gang's shown up," the Bronx police lieutenant, fifty-three, informed his men at their daily meeting, "Wilde, Whitman, Genet, Gide, Albee, and, get this, *Coward*—they been spray-painting their names *everywhere*";

a gambler, fifty-five, lost a round of "pitz," the deadly Mayan ball game, in a Yorkville basement and needed to be rescued by the superheroine Lorna Liebmilch, who told him, "I'm here to help";

while gazing up at Grand Central Station for the first time, a woman, forty-two, told her sister, "Now *that's* impressive," and the sister, forever cryptic, responded by saying, "You oughta see it when they fill this place with water";

a conspiracy theorist, thirty-nine, surprised a friend by saying, "Actually, the JFK assassination was not due to any group plan—Oswald was just a loner misogynist who was aiming his rifle at Jackie";

"Don't get too down on yourself," the jeet kune do instructor, fifty-one, told his class, "because there's always somebody better than you," but when a student asked, "What about the one person who's *best*—not perfect, no, but statistically the best?" the instructor mulled this over, then said, "That person's getting old";

while skimming through a magazine, a man, forty-four, learned of his celebrity ex-classmate's divorce—her husband had battered her—and now he murmured to himself, "She shouldn't have turned me down at Rutgers";

"When I was sixteen," a woman, thirty, told a new friend at a diner, "my mom and I were doing laundry and something she said pissed me off so much that I wished she would drop dead, and then and there she had a brain hemorrhage and *did* die—so, yeah,

I guess I've got issues"; a man, fifty, who'd slept poorly last night, accidentally brushed his teeth with diaper rash cream;

"Take this gun and practice in the mirror," said the boyfriend of a woman, twenty-two, but next Tuesday at a Chase bank in Brooklyn her words would come out as "Fuck for the sky, you motherstickers, this is a *reachup!*";

a woman, forty-eight, scolded a ghost who occupied her new home, saying, "*I* live here now, not *you*," which made the ghost vanish from sight, although the woman would still sometimes feel that ghost sitting on her bed and notice an indentation made by an invisible rump;

Ahasuerus, the Wandering Jew, looked deep into his new chiropractor's eyes, whose odd blue color, the immortal realized, precisely matched "*hsbd-iryt*," the type of pigment first created in ancient Egypt;

on being told that an acquaintance's star sign was Leo, Baron Samedi, voodoo lord of the dead, exclaimed with delight, "Wow, so is mine! Aren't we lions *wonderful*?";

a newborn girl, having received total knowledge of the world while in the womb, was lightly struck on her upper lip by an angel so she'd forget everything she'd learned;

and a taxi driver, thirty-seven, who would spend the rest of his life saying, "People blame me but it not my *fault*, it not my *fault*, I never *hear* of no John Lennons," stopped for a thickset dark-haired young man who clutched a paperback and a record album and who said, once he got settled in the cab, "The Dakota, please—and step on it."

MURDER IN MY HEART FOR BOSCO HUTCHINS

When I said no to the homeless man who'd flagged down my car on the quiet Miami street one night and demanded money from me, he got angry and pressed his fists against his forehead and yelled, "I'm using my psychic powers to make you croak by early next week," and for a moment I thought about running him over, consequences be damned, just to tell by the look on his face as he went under my wheels if those "psychic powers" of his had allowed him to predict his fate.

MY WEAKNESS IS NONE OF YOUR BUSINESS (2)

Old Ulrich was a rake, bearing scars on both his thighs from the time when he was sitting on the toilet at home and his wife, having just learned of his latest infidelity, rushed into the bathroom with a knife and slashed at his penis—which she would have cut off, too, had he not leaned back and lifted his legs just in time for his thighs to bear the brunt of the blow meant for his master.

BIBLIOMANIAS

"Why have you spent your whole adult life taking college courses?" Pryna asked the old man, who'd studied law, medicine, physics, forestry, medieval European literature, mathematics, modern art history, architecture, US military history, Japanese samurai armor, the life of Francis Marion ("Swamp Fox of the American Revolution"), macroeconomics, and microeconomics, with some home economics thrown in, and the old man's answer was, "Because I didn't want to be like my grandfather, who read the same book, *Fishing Camps I Have Known*, in our public library every day for forty years."

IN A PERHAPS
MORE FERLINGHETTIAN WORLD

Fortune has its cookies to give out, as Ferlinghetti taught us, and other baked goods, as well, so picture my surprise when I glance through my window and find a squirrel looking at me with a bagel in its paws, then imagine my disappointment when I dash outside with my camera to find that the squirrel has disappeared, and now imagine my delight when I hear wings and a "*caw-caw-caw*" sound right above me and I look up to find a raven flying off with that just-stolen bagel—or, in a better world, a different bagel that's just as tasty.

**"HIGH-BACKED WOLF," "LIMBER LANCE,"
"LEFT-HAND SHOOTER," "WOODEN LEG,"
"BRIGHT SUN MAKER," "ROMAN NOSE,"
"COYOTE DROPPINGS," "BLACK MOON,"
"BAD FACE," "PLENTY COUPS," "DRY
THROAT," "SIX FEATHERS," "BLOODY
KNIFE," "CROW KING," "CUT BELLY," "BIG
PRISONER," "LOOKING GLASS," "SHAVE
HEAD," "SKY CHIEF," "THUNDER MAN," "ONE
BRAID," "STIFF NECK," "FIAT WAR CLUB,"
"KIT FOX," "HUSH-HUSH-CUTE," AND
"TIMBERED MOUNTAIN"**

Such were the Native American–style names that Kenneth secretly assigned to each of his friends—"secretly," because he'd always felt ashamed of his grandmother's Lenni Lenape blood (she never got to teach him that the one thing wrong with Whites is that they can't be Indians)—and when death found him, in a multiplex near Lincoln Park, death felt easy for Kenneth to bear because he knew he'd finally made it, no one had unmasked him, and now his true self, that secret bad self, would pass away with him forever.

TOWER OF REUBEN

Because my father kept *Everything You Always Wanted to Know About Sex* (*But Were Afraid to Ask)* by David S. Reuben, MD on the highest shelf of his library, I needed to stack three chairs to build a tower to stand on to reach that goal, but just as I opened the book, the tower wobbling, my nosy stepmother appeared out of thin air and screeched, "What's going *on* here?" (thus anticipating a witty teacher some years later who would catch me cheating on an exam and screech, "Looks like I caught you with your pants down and your knowledge hanging out")—and in a metaphorical sense I'm still atop that wobbly tower, getting busted while striving to explore Reuben's Great Mystery.

LIQUORED UP AND LACQUERED DOWN

"I've never felt so happy in my life," the young woman mumbles as Lou Reed sings "I Love You, Suzanne" from her Sony Walkman, and the five-sided room in this hostel spins crazily around her, and the *Kirs Royales* splosh about inside her, and the blood from her accidentally cut forearm drips all over her, and the strangers in her bed, trying to sleep, all holler, "Shut up," and here in Paris she's doubly blessed, for she's unable to foresee that, though she'll come close once or twice, she'll never feel such happiness again.

DOES ALFRED E.
NEUMAN HAVE A BROTHER?

"Your old man's a good boss," red-haired Georgy told me each time we took the company truck to deliver toilets to local plumbers, and after he accidentally drove that truck straight into the Newark Bar Supply Store, wrecking the building and injuring one employee, Georgy said, "I don't blame your old man for firing me, but I don't feel so guilty, neither, 'cause God forgives *whatever* I do, which makes me like that goofball in *MAD* magazine, my fellow redhead, who's keeps on saying, '*What, me worry?*'"

CHOCOLATE (2)

"We think you're great," the brunette sisters told the author at his reading at Book Soup as they handed him a chocolate box, which he accepted with a smile, politely not mentioning to them that he'd given up eating sugar, but the next morning on his flight home his sugar craving overwhelmed him, so he pulled the chocolate box out of his backpack, opened the lid (*Just one*, he promised himself), and found not chocolate inside that box but a door key, along with this note: "*Hotel Ofotert, Suite 47—We're waiting for you.*"

"How do you feel about *apes*?" asked my taxi driver, and before I could answer, he was telling me of how he'd once been hired to drive a small gorilla from an airport to a zoo—"Their zoo truck was full already," he said, "so they paid me two hundred bucks for a fifty dollar fare, and I said, 'Sure,' because, hey, even if that ape took a crap here, I figured the extra dough would make it worth it, and, besides, they promised me they *drugged* the thing, which must be why it just *sat* there next to where you're sitting, pal, not moving much or being noisy, all it did was stare out the window and scarf down these bananas they gave it, peels and all, that ape just popped them in its mouth like they was gumdrops, and in the end, no, it didn't shit up my cab, thank fucking God, but it *did* leave behind this *stench*, this smell you *just* would not believe, I couldn't get it out *for weeks*, I scrubbed and scrubbed and couldn't beat it, all my customers complained, and in the end I had to pay some fancy company to clean that seat, they made me pay them through the teeth, so I lost money on the deal, but at least it's finally gone, I haven't smelled that stench in months"—and as he went on I was thinking, *I could smell it just as soon as I sat down here, which means your ape, wherever* else *he is, might as well be sitting right beside me.*

153

THE TALE OF THE ARCHER'S WIFE

While his wife watched, the archer stood on his Westport lawn and sent his latest arrow on its way, but not only did that feathered shaft miss the bull's-eye, it missed the whole target, whistling instead through the skies above this world, where it cut raindrops in half, smashed snowflakes, dodged every hailstone, grazed the wing of a young crane, entered and exited too many clouds to count and then, after circling the globe, whistled back to Westport, where it headed for the soft back of the archer, who stood wondering where his arrow went while his wife, having noticed its destination, began to laugh.

QUETZALCOATL'S CHOICE

Last night in Mexico City, the reigning champion was a sphinx perched on a ring post, licking its chops, the challenger was a phoenix who jogged to-and-fro through a ring of fire, and you were the referee, explaining to them, "I want a good clean fight, guys, with no spitting," but just before the bell rang, a screaming came across the sky in the Meineke Muffler Pavilion, big feathers fluttering everywhere (with some of them so razor edged that they beheaded audience members), and a giant feathered serpent, the Aztec god Quetzalcoatl, landed right inside the ring and gobbled down both combatants.

WAY OUT WEST: A DOUBLE PLAY

Accounts differ as to what goodies Mephistopheles promised Faust in exchange for that mortal's immortal soul—was it supreme knowledge, or a quasar ride, or just a medieval serving of mindless fun?—but I happen to know that what Faust most desired was the ability to shape a whole geographical region, which in this case was the nineteenth century American West, where Faust conjured up cowboys, Indians, gunslingers, stagecoach drivers, train robbers, silver miners, cardsharps, drunk sawbones, saloon gals, and sheriffs, with each sheriff perfectly resembling Faust himself because, ever since his turbulent childhood, he'd felt the need to tame every possible kind of chaos.

⁂

"Mr. Wayne," said the precocious nine-year-old who was meeting for her first time a famous person—in this case, the towering movie cowboy who now wore a toupee instead of his Stetson—"Mr. Wayne, on behalf of the American public, I'd like to thank you for the many years of entertainment you've given us," and even though the girl would grow up to learn about and despise that movie cowboy's fascist worldview, she'd secretly go on cherishing the memory of their meeting.

ANOTHER FLASHING CHANCE AT BLISS

Near the Paris apartment where the singer Jim Morrison supposedly died, Map met a young Tunisian woman with diabetes who said, "I wish I could have made sex with Jim," so Map told her, "Ten years ago in New York, I, uh, 'made sex' with someone who claimed she lost her virginity to Morrison, so I might be as close as you'll get to your dream lover," and lo and behold, the woman on hearing this gave Map a soulful kiss and invited him to her home, but all she ended up doing there was make him watch as she injected herself with insulin.

A NON-GOLFER READS GOLF MAGAZINE

Pregnant at sixteen, she felt lost, didn't know what she should do until, while seated in her doctor's waiting room, she found direction—and, with that, calm—from the front cover of the June edition of *Golf* Magazine—specifically, the story title "Let Nature Take Its Courses"—and so today, a decade later, unsure if she should marry a man named Kent (he's far from perfect, but always wonderful with her son), she goes to a newsstand and buys the latest *Golf*, which says "Go for Broke!" on its cover.

LADIES AND GENTLEMEN, UNCLE NORBERT!

Sunk in upon himself in his wheelchair and long past being able to hear or speak to us, Uncle Norbert raised his right hand from his lap in slow motion, so we watched in silence as that hand moved toward his face, wondering the whole time if he would use it to mop his brow, or scratch his cheek, or even wipe away a tear, but, no—what Norbert finally did was stick a finger in his nostril and root around there.

TRITON'S CHOICE

Although he'd written a song called "Let the Mermaids Flirt with Me," the great bluesman Mississippi John Hurt had never seen an ocean until the day his young friend Maria brought him to Martha's Vineyard, where John spent hours on the beach just watching surfers, a preoccupation he later explained by saying, "I didn't spot no mermaids, naw, but I sure did like to see them folks go riding on their wave-saddles."

A HEART WITH EXTRA MUSCLE

During a day flight from Madrid, the tall and well-built old stranger seated beside me spoke of his life, how he'd served in Naval Intelligence in World War II, won bodybuilding championships in the fifties, and finally lived for decades as the common-law husband of a much older movie icon, a woman he still mourned deeply but wouldn't name—"Let's not discuss her," he said, "it's just too painful"—and so, the next day, following a hunch, I went to a library and found a book about a certain movie icon and opened it to the photo section where there he was, younger and happier, with a brawny arm wrapped around his wife Mae West.

GO HOME AND DIG IT!

158   After they lost their child, the heartsick newlyweds drove to Durango, where they stole a lifelike baby doll from a Woolworths, then sat cradling it and cooing to it at a high school football game, and at game's end they hurled that doll onto the playing field and shouted at the losing team words they'd stolen from the writer Barry Hannah: "Buck up now, boys, and love the loss just like the gain, because we saw victory and defeat here, and both were wonderful, and no one died."

A DUNE BUGGY BUILT FOR TWO

Met David through mutual friend in the nineties; dinners together at an East Village diner; the first published novelist close to my age who took an interest in my work; gave compliments, too ("I want to be your authorized biographer"); told crazy tales from his own life (dune buggy accident and resulting month-long coma which he spent talking with Roy Orbison, who'd died the day the coma started); then one mild jokey insult I took offense to and I ghosted him, never speaking to David again; decades of silence till I read his brief *Times* obit (an aneurysm—dune buggy legacy?); and now his novels reproach me from my bookshelf, saying, "Why take offense at one mild jokey insult?"; and if he's anywhere I hope he's back again with Roy and Roy's giving David singing lessons.

"CSILLOG A FENY"

Something about the stuffed toy, a cute pink octopus, was urging Map to buy it, so he took it home from the Upper East Side *tchotchkes* shop and left it in a corner of his living room, where the toy sat ignored by Map and all his guests until one day three decades later when a friend of his came to visit and she brought along her grandson, a child suffering from leukemia, and as soon as this child beheld the toy he shouted "*Octopus*" and ran to it and hugged it tight, prompting Map's friend to say, "I'm sorry" and Map to answer, "No, don't worry, it belongs to the boy, it always *has*—I just didn't realize that till now."

STANDARD NIPPLE WORKS

Sing, o Muse, of my father Buddy, a plumber, who was a most incurious man, so much so that when I told him the title of this story—I'd taken it from the name of a plumbing supply warehouse in our town—he did not say, "Why would you call a story *that*?" but simply nodded his head and informed me, "I used to buy toilets from them."

LET THE SKY RAIN PLANTAINS

While bopping along Spring Street, Pryna came upon a boy who was weeping as only children can, with the boy's grandmother unable to console him, so Pryna took a fake million dollar bill from her wallet and gave it to the kid, saying, "Buck up, you newly minted millionaire you," which dried those tears fast, and later on, Pryna was in the subway where she beheld another weeping child, a girl whose father was ignoring her, so Pryna thought, *To the rescue again I go* and handed the girl another fake million, but instead of welcoming it, the girl just tore the bill to shreds and wept even harder, which caused her father to slap her face, twice, then shout at Pryna, "Stay the fuck away from my Debbie!"

WHO LOST IT AT THE MOVIES?:
A TRIPLE PLAY

"Let's go see a movie," my mother would say each weekend, and off we'd drive to the nearest suburban cinema, though she would never check when our film was due to start, so we'd walk in at the middle or at the end (very rarely the beginning), and we would have to figure out which character was which, and who'd done what, and the reasons they did it, which might explain why stories, even banal ones, now seem so compelling to me.

⁘

Another thing about my childhood moviegoing: if there was a sex scene in a film we saw, my mother would grimace, snarling, "Such *filth*," and drag me out of that cinema by my elbow, not even bothering to get her money back, which might explain why sex, even the most mundane sex, now seems so transgressive to me.

⁘

Entering one movie theater in the middle of a Clint Eastwood picture, my mother and I realized that we'd walked in right during a sex scene, so she grimaced, snarling, "Such *filth*," and dragged me out of there—but *this* time the audience heard her and laughed, mocking us, which might explain why, to this day, I can't bear to see any movies with Clint Eastwood.

CONSOLATION FOR THE BALD

Only after the hair-loss specialist touched my bald skull and in a weird flat voice said, "It's too late, I can't help you" did I suddenly recall a night four decades back when a young woman at a college party answered my question "Wanna dance?" by saying, in a voice as weird and flat as that hair doctor's, "No, not with *you*"—so now I know that none of our memories are ever lost, they're all still planted in our bald heads and simply waiting to grow out.

TILL THERE WAS EUBIE

Back in the seventies I loved to wander around Washington Square Park with my friends and listen to Eubie, this middle-aged Black street singer who had a strong pleading voice as he sang pop tunes like "Till There Was You," but come the eighties Eubie vanished, no one knew where he had gone, then one evening in '92 when I was visiting Berlin, strolling along the Ku'damm, I heard a familiar voice and, wow, here he was, looking older but still crooning "Till There Was You," and after Eubie finished his set I told him I knew him from New York and gave him whatever *Deutschmarks* I could spare and asked him why he was in Germany, so he answered, "It was the *Jews*, man, those goddamn *Jews*, they burned me out of Staten Island, stole all my bread, so I came *here* where everybody *understands* me, they know how to handle Jews in this town, just *gas them all*, I'm a black Nazi," and once I got over my shock at hearing this, I said, "But *I'm* Jewish," and instead of looking sour, Eubie touched my shoulder, saying, "So I guess you're one of them *good Jews*, I've met a few," and in a rage now, I slapped away his hand and shouted at him words that strike me now as childish but which I meant with all my heart: "Good luck with your fellow Nazis, you asshole, but just remember we already beat you in *two* world wars, and if you start your shit again, *we'll finish you off*."

LARCENY-HEARTED ME

"My closest brush with death," said the silver-haired man who'd prowled down 1970s fashion runways like a panther, "was the day when I was sitting in a taxi and a steel girder that accidentally fell from a construction project way above me crashed through my taxi's roof, plunged into the vinyl seat beside my leg, then buried itself in Wilshire Boulevard, basically *impaling* that taxi, pinning it into the street but leaving me unharmed," and when I said, "What a crazy story," he snapped, "Don't you steal it, Mr. Writer, because I'm saving it for my memoirs."

ARROW TO BULL'S-EYE

When I die, I'll bet my ghost will circle back to my nursery school in Elizabeth, that red brick building where I would wait in a hallway after lunch, a half-day student because I couldn't bear to be without my mother for too long, and when at last she pulled up in her Chevy convertible, smooth and white with red upholstery, our teacher would call my name and I would dash down the staircase and out the front door and straight to that car, arrow to bull's-eye, shouting "Mommy" with such feeling that nothing since has really matched it—yes, *here* my ghost will probably wind up, drifting high above that schoolyard, watching this scene play out again, again, again, until the wind rises up to whisk away all things on earth, including ghosts.

ENDLESS BOOGIE

Thanks to Map's high fever, and to the three rats scampering around at his feet, and to the seven snoring, farting, grunting fellow travelers crammed in the fifth-class compartment with him, and to the multitude of bad odors swirling all around, he didn't sleep a wink on last night's train, but once dawn broke and they arrived in New Delhi and Map staggered through the station, his fever spiking, and found a taxi to bring him to his usual hotel, the manager at the front desk said, "You're always so nice to our staff so we've upgraded you to our Presidential Suite," thereby providing Map with his life's two most *different* consecutive nights—at least in terms of comfort.

POINT YOUR PINKIE TO THE NORTH STAR

Here's a story about Pryna and her Israeli lover, who spent six hours with their thumbs out on the highway from Eilat until a hydro-engineer stopped in his truck and said, "I'll drive you to Masada" (which is where they hoped to go) "if you'll stay at my water station tonight and help me run tests," and even though this sounded weird, the couple said yes, and now, forty years on, what Pryna remembers even more than Masada or her lover is how she'd worked as a scientist's aide, lowering an empty bucket by rope into the Dead Sea, hearing a splash, then yanking up the now-heavy bucket to check the water's salination, doing this process over and over until the darkness gave way to dawn.

A PIRATE'S LIFE FOR ME

As middle age tilts into old age, my mind's been misplacing certain memories, making me fear they're irretrievable ("What terrifies us most about death," someone's said, "is not the loss of the future, it's the loss of the past"), but today I heard Gordon Lightfoot's "Steel Rail Blues," a song I hadn't thought of for ages, and the sound of it shot me back as if from a cannon to the summer night forty years ago when my friend Jim and I woke at dawn in Virginia after driving all night and then sleeping in my Nova's front seat, and the sunshine in the green field where we'd parked felt like a blessing, and despite my bleary eyes and cottony mouth and aching head, a pirate's life of high excitement now stretched before us—we'd never die, or at least not age (all we needed was a Jolly Roger bumper sticker)—and when I popped into the tape deck our cassette of *Lightfoot's Best*, that song "Steel Rail Blues" seemed unforgettable, which, surprise, it's so far proved to be.

I'M HAPPY AND I'M SINGING AND A 1, 2, 3, 4

Back in my hotel room, the Egyptian-American woman Zhania spoke of her violent father, her zoned-out-on-Valium mother, and how she'd left home at sixteen, determined to be an actress, although aside from some body-double work on TV (that's her foot kicking some guy's groin during a *Baywatch* episode), the acting didn't work out, so Zhania drifted home to Boston and started stripping, which made sense because she liked to drive around late at night with no clothes on, a hobby, she said, that made her feel, for some reason, "like, *immortal*."

AFTER-LIFERS

You always assumed that when we die, it's straight oblivion or else we shift to a higher plane and learn the answers to all our questions, but then Pryna wrecked this either-or jazz by saying, "Even if there *is* an afterlife where every mystery is solved, maybe we won't qualify for that—we're not significant enough, or don't deserve it—and so, while elephants or dolphins or even ETs might win that big prize, all *we* get is just 'lights out.'"

SOMEONE'S USED-TO-BE

The beautiful woman told Map halfway through their blind date, "I'm still crazy about my ex-boyfriend, though he would always get disturbed when we made love, saying, 'Something feels *different* down there,' so I explained, 'I had an appendectomy that went wrong,' and I should've *kept* feeding him this lie, too, because he ditched me right after I finally told the truth, which is that before my reassignment surgery I used to be a man."

LADIES AND GENTLEMEN, UNCLE MO!

The Perlmutters stopped inviting Uncle Mo to family functions after he ate half of Joel's nose at the boy's Bar Mitzvah—the nose, that is, on a chopped-liver sculpture they'd commissioned of their son—and after Mo kept begging them for "a chance to make it right," they at last gave in and invited him to their daughter Jane's Bat Mitzvah, where Mo brought along a pork chop that he tossed into the punchbowl.

THE STORY OF MY LIFE
IN 200 WORDS OR LESS

According to my father, I was cooked up in a tourist hotel in San Juan, where Puerto Rico's scents and sounds must have wafted into my mother's womb to marinate me;

then one night, decades later, in the dark and empty lobby of a youth hostel in San Juan (my only visit to Puerto Rico as of yet), I gasped when I beheld a ghost, although this ghost turned out to be a young albino with whom I ended up making love on the lobby's scratchy carpet (and since we didn't use a condom, we may have cooked up a child that night, with this child still out there somewhere, already grown);

and now I imagine that when I die, Stretchfoot (which is Death's medieval nickname because he "stretches the limbs of the dying") will give me a piggyback ride back to San Juan, where he'll repeal the laws of time, reduce me to one molecule, and then insert me in my mother as she makes love with my father, thereby starting this 178-word life story once again.

MIRACLES HAPPEN TO THOSE WHO BELIEVE IN THEM

Gone are the days when we'd drink bourbon at *Leche Vin*, a joint near the Bastille where Christian icons filled the walls and where a drunk legionnaire at the bar snarled, "Five hundred *francs* says you can't turn this water into wine," so you said "*Deal*" and, when the legionnaire's head was turned, you reached under your skirt and pulled a Tampon out of yourself and briefly dipped it in the glass, turning that water red and prompting the legionnaire to chug it down and then say, "Lousy stuff, but yeah, it's wine, so here's your *francs*, you little miracle-maker you."

FUCKING LIGHTNING

"Fucking lightning," said a stout man at the campfire that night, "I heard a story where a bolt of it wrecked someone's front door, cut that whole sucker in half, as if to warn the family cowering behind it, '*Nowhere to hide*,'" which led a younger man to say, "Oh, I've heard worse, like how a bolt came through a ceiling, ignored the parents who were lying in their bed, and aimed directly for their child who they were cuddling between themselves as if they thought they could protect him."

OH, WHAT A BLOW THAT PHANTOM DEALT ME

"Whoa, I'm sorry," I told the old man on the toilet in the diner's tiny bathroom when I accidentally walked in on him, but "*Wait*," he cried, and then I realized he was *me*, my own self many years from now, the eighty-something-year-old Gary—or a Gary I *might* become—and when he said, "Don't make the error that *I* made, you must accept that piece of paper a guy named Charles will give to you in Loomis Park on April 18, 2030," I had no idea what he meant, so I just said another "Sorry" and walked back to my table, having decided to hold it in till I got home.

PARIS IN SPRINGTIME WITH CARLOS

Paranoia was like mother's milk to Hopp, so on a spring day in '88 when he stood on the Metro reading a biography of Carlos Ramirez, the so-called "Jackal," at that time the world's most wanted terrorist, a woman with a harelip said to Hopp, "How dare you read about that great man, you're not fit to say his name, I promise you that you won't leave Paris alive," and thanks to this threat, Hopp spent the next days in a panic, convinced that everyone he met was either a Carlos ally or else Carlos himself in drag, Hopp never guessing that the woman with the harelip was just a trickster who liked to improvise however possible to freak out strangers.

PARIS IN SPRINGTIME
WITH CARLOS: THE SEQUEL

Although the trickster regretted that her pranks often caused suffering, she simply couldn't control herself, and so she went on playing those tricks until the day of a Halloween parade near Les Halles when she mischievously told a policeman, "Cool costume, dude" right before a moon-walking Michael Jackson imitator exploded, killing dozens, injuring our trickster, and proving that the Jackal, Carlos Ramirez, still loved his work.

THIS BOXER'S BEGINNING

Map felt so ashamed of how winded he got during his first boxing lesson that he lied to his instructor, claiming he had asthma, but this tactic backfired because the instructor said, "If you got asthma, then you gotta get permission from a doctor before we go on," so Map made an appointment with an internist who trained at the same gym, although in her office she kept Map waiting for so long that when he finally got to see her, he yelled, "You wasted my *time!*" at the doctor, whose temper was even worse than Map's and who knocked Map out with a good right hook.

HONEY, COME QUICK WITH THE IODINE

In the early eighties we were the only White kids who drank at "Three J's," a tavern in our old town where the friendly owner said, "The name means 'Jukin', Jivin' and Jrinkin'," but one night when we brought along our pretty blond friend Darla, the owner stopped being friendly and said, "You better get that blondie outta here or someone gonna get *cut*"—and who knows now what became of Three J's, and who knows what became of Darla, but tonight I'm looking at a big bright yellow half-moon over my new town, and I'm thinking, *It looks like someone cut* you, *blondie.*

HOW TO GET DIVERTED

Every time you planned to take your life, you got diverted by one thing or another—a terribly disabled person who staggered past you made you think, *If she can do it, so can I*, and hearing "Moon River" on the radio in your dentist's office made you think, *If I die, I'll never get to hear this gorgeous melody again*— but the weirdest "diversion" happened the night you were rushing to your drugstore to buy enough drugs for an overdose and you stopped when you noticed a sheet of paper stuck on a tree branch—it was just impaled there, who knew why?— and on this paper someone had scribbled the command "BE HAPPY" which was followed by the words, "*zucchini, mussels, hemp hearts, chopped meat, pepper, sugar, olive oil*," which made you think, *This is so odd that I guess I'll* try *to "be happy"—for one more day, at least*, and this day led to other days, and after a week you noticed the name of the new grocery store on your block, which was "Jah Victor's 'Be Happy' Food Mart."

CARLO ZENO, IF YOU PLEASE:
A DOUBLE PLAY

"Remember Carlo Zeno," our optimistic friend Irv would say whenever life looked really bleak, and if someone said, "Who?" he'd explain, "In the 1370s, the Genoese navy blockaded Venice, so the *doge* sent pleas for help to a native son, the rogue admiral Carlo Zeno, but months went by and no help came and all seemed lost until, just before the Venetians surrendered, they spotted familiar sails on the horizon, and as the historian Hazlitt put it, so excited he used all caps, 'IT WAS CARLO ZENO WHO HAD COME AT LAST, AND VENICE WAS INDEED SAVED.'"

One summer in Paris I felt so depressed that my only joy came from listening to a pop song, "Find The Answer Within" by the Boo Radleys, and when I learned that this group was due to play an outdoor concert at the Bastille, I hurried there yet showed up too late, just as the group were leaving the stage—"*C'est finis*," an old woman confirmed to me—so I broke down and started crying, feeling worse than ever now, but then the group came back and said, "We're gonna play *one more* for you, Paris!" and when they launched into that last song, *my* song, the song "Find The Answer Within," I took the hands of the old woman and started dancing, dancing like mad, and the ghost of Carlo Zeno might as well have been there, too, saying, "Yes, remember me."

SISTER DELANEY'S LIP-SMACKIN' SOUL FOOD KITCHEN

"I'm a good cook, so do you know who I can speak to about me starting my own restaurant here?" a destitute-looking woman asked a security guard at a shopping mall's food court, and after the guard pointed to the mall's management office, a customer who'd overheard her told the woman something that made her smile (and made the destitute-looking child who held her hand smile, too): "I'm looking forward to trying your food, ma'am."

SAINT DEATH VS. CINDY

Halfway through their first date, Map described his new book project to Cindy, saying, "It's about the narco-gangsters who worship '*Santa Muerte*,'" but it occurred to him that he would be getting no second date when Cindy said, "Yeah, well, I'm *not* so into death, because when I was six and watching TV with my parents, some junkie climbed through our window and told my father she wanted money and even after he gave it to her, she shot him dead in front of us."

FANGS OF ROSY FLINT: A DOUBLE PLAY

At age five, a boy named Remo Chiti sat in a Miami Beach hotel room watching a TV horror rerun in which a Haitian zombie called Bredda Gravalicious marauded around stabbing people from behind, prompting Remo to shout "*Mama!*" and to never sleep again on his stomach because his back needed protection from zombie knives.

Asked by a journalist how much he loved his current wife, Remo, now a famous TV actor, said, "So much so that when some young thug snatched her purse on the Strand in London, I ran after him for three blocks"—not mentioning that after those three blocks the thief got tired of being chased, spun around, pulled out a knife, and now began to chase Remo, who shouted "*Mama!*" as he ran, calling out for help from the true love of his life.

SHORTIES: A DESSERT BAR WITH SWEETBLOOD TEA

"Let it out," hollered the young woman from Dresden, smacking my hand away from the beer mug in which I'd playfully trapped an annoying wasp, and only later, once she'd gone home, did the friend who'd introduced us explain to me, "She refused to be a Stasi informer so they locked her up for three years and now she can't stand seeing prisons, even small ones."

~~~

Every time Pryna visited her Norwegian cousins in their village on a fjord, she would gaze at a strange bare spot on the side of a nearby mountain and wonder about it until she remembered (why did Pryna always forget this?) that a neighboring village had occupied that bare spot for centuries until 1969 (her birth year, of all the years), when an avalanche destroyed it.

~~~

"The worst part about death," the bedridden man said to Map at the hospice where Map worked, "is how it's like your favorite soap opera is getting cancelled, so you can't find out what happens next," but before Map got to ask him, "'Next' in *the* world or 'next' in *your* world?" the other patient in the room, another goner, switched on the TV with his remote and jacked the volume way up high.

~~~

I disliked the obnoxious Australian businessman from the moment I met him at a party, and I disliked him even more once we discovered through some listless small talk that we shared the same birthdate in the same year, making us the same age exactly, but my dislike for this man changed to pity when I found his name and face in a book about the 9/11 victims.

❊

At the Belly Button Biodiversity Project, test subject Pryna Pamlig learned that she had 2,378 species of bacteria in her navel while her then-boyfriend, test subject Map Grylapin, was found to possess in his "innie" a microbe never recorded outside Japan—which is how Pryna discovered that Map, who could never get away with *shit*, was cheating on her with her friend Yuki.

❊

"I've gotten married," my Parisian ex-girlfriend announced when we met again after eight years over tea at our favorite café, but when I said, "Congrats, I'd like to meet the lucky guy" (wishing, in fact, that it had been me instead), she smiled, saying, "Oh, that's not possible, because my husband is Jesus Christ."

❊

During your first few moments of walking around New Delhi, you were gazing up at an impressive building when you stepped in something gooey on the sidewalk, something you feared was either dog shit, or cow shit, or elephant shit, or even human shit, but when you queasily looked down to find out just what kind it was, you saw not shit but an unmarked patch of wet cement already hardening around your sneakers.

❊

When my father at age eighty showed me the yellowed pages that featured "Going Home for Christmas," a tale he'd scrawled in pencil as a ten-year-old schoolboy, I thought, *He and I aren't so different from the Yuletide plane-crash survivors in his story—strangers with little in common who nevertheless get forced together by circumstance and now are trying as hard as they can to make the best of it.*

⁂

"In my next life, I want to be someone like you," Map told the famous old composer, whom he'd hero-worshipped for years, but her response made clear to Map how unenlightened he had been: "In my next life," said the composer, "I want to be someone like me."

⁂

Said the old high-wire walker—who, ironically enough, had stumbled at the lecture hall when he'd stepped forward to warmly greet us—"When I was young, I wore a skull-and-crossbones ring to remind me of my fate, but then I wised up and got rid of that ring and now I wear a shirt with a silk square on my shoulder so that whenever I succeed at something, I slap the square, giving myself a symbolic 'pat on the back.'"

⁂

"We just like it this way," the married couple tells anyone who asks why their bed is built so high above their floor, requiring a ladder to reach it, but the truth, which they're embarrassed to divulge, is that they find graveyards impersonal and so they bury their dead relatives right beneath their sleeping selves.

⁂

"Yes, I *did* get ill during my recent trip to India, quite sick to my stomach," said the English bishop who sat beside you on a night flight, "and at first I thought the problem was caused by my drinking from a fountain where beggars washed themselves, but then I reminded myself that this dirty water was *holy water*, water I'd blessed before I drank it, so my illness must have come from all that spicy food I ate."

Whenever I walk past the corner of Sixty-Fifth and Broadway, I remember standing there on a night thirty years ago and speaking with my friend Scott, neither one of us suspecting he would die a few days later, and now I wish that when he'd *kvetched* to me about his latest failed romance, I'd interrupted him to say, "Forget that, man—just look up and dig *the stars!*" (although you couldn't see any stars from there, and still can't).

ᴧᴧᴧᴧᴧ

"Yes," said the Inuit elder, "we *do* have such people who you call '*psych-o-path*,' but as soon as we notice that a person behaves this way, we take him on a seal hunt where one of our men, who has agreed to save the tribe from danger, will leap forward to club and then drown this, this—*what* was that word you used again?"

ᴧᴧᴧᴧᴧ

At your first bullfight, in Barcelona, you found it cute to cheer on the bull until the moment when it gored the matador, which made you feel guilty, so at your next bullfight, in Puerto Vallarta, you declared yourself neutral and just enjoyed the show until the bull jumped over the wall you sat behind and gored you.

ᴧᴧᴧᴧᴧ

"One of the sights I'd like to see here in Bergen is the thousand-year-old wooden stave church," I told the typically tall Norwegian bartender, who said, "Too late—some Satanists burned down that church last night," which made me laugh at this joke till I remembered smelling wood-smoke when I'd arrived in town that morning, and I realized that this bartender was dead serious.

Dorothy Parker said, "People change and forget to tell each other," but when Pryna's friend Hepzibah joined the new cult of "Gastrologos," which posits that our food communicates with our subconscious minds as we digest it, Hepzibah kept trying to recruit Pryna to her cult, never shutting up about it, thereby—in this case, at least—proving Parker wrong.

While dining alone next to a silent elderly couple at a Burmese restaurant, I thought, *They've run out of things to say to each other, like all-too-many married people,* but when one of the two, the wife, finally spoke, what she said was addressed not to her husband but to me (although they shared a naughty smile): "It must feel *lonely,* your eating dinner all by yourself, hmmm?"

What strange chairs, I thought about the boulder-sized lumps of fabric that dotted the otherwise empty marble floor of the Hindu temple near Agra, but when I began to sit on one, exhausted from my busy day as a tourist, the chair came to life beneath me, changing shape and making a grunting sound, at which point I realized that these were not chairs but blanket-covered worshippers.

Map was surprised when a strange woman took a jar of peanut butter from her satchel, dipped her hand in it, and then finger-painted strange symbols on an elm tree in Union Square, but this was nothing compared to how surprised Map was when, fifteen minutes later, a strange man approached that tree as if he knew what he would find there and began to lick away those symbols.

So there I was, walking through Copenhagen's freetown of Christiania with a biker I'd just met, a burly guy I later learned was wanted for murder, when a small man with a big plate of French fries caught sight of my new friend, yelped out loud, tossed those French fries in the air, and ran off, which made the biker laugh and say, "He owes me money."

When the elevator reached the Vegas hotel's lobby, the famous porn actress, accompanied by her bodyguards, walked ahead of Pryna and hurried past a bona fide Amish family who'd been waiting to board that elevator, so Pryna thought, while shaking her head in awe, *I may never again see such different American archetypes occupy the same small patch of universe.*

The woman who bought my childhood home from me seemed quite normal until the closing, where in the presence of our realtors and our lawyers she announced, "I can't wait to move in with my twenty-seven cats, they'll *love* it there, but don't worry, Gary, I'll keep your bedroom just how it was so you can come back whenever you want and stay with us and pretend I'm your big sister."

"My father, he was one tough Pole, a Mob enforcer," said Cousin Sam's beefy nurse, who seemed pretty tough herself, "and when I was a kid, Papa would bring me to work with him—at this church in Passaic, for instance, where the minister owed gambling debts, and so I sat in a pew reading the funnies while Papa hung him from a cross and punched his stomach till that minister finally said, 'Take the collection box, it's full.'"

Lost in a sand-storm at the desert music festival, I finally happened upon a woman who wore a bikini and a gas mask—*Great*, I thought, *help at last*—but she didn't move a muscle or say a word when I asked her for directions, so I asked again, to no avail, and I felt angry at being dissed till I stepped closer and saw that someone had left their mannequin behind here.

As soon as you heard that Tenderloins, the shop where you've been buying your underwear for forty years, would soon shut down forever, you bought their entire stock in your size—"This amount'll last you a *lifetime*," the salesman joked—and you realized he could be right, because for the first time in your life, you perhaps just did something (something as mundane yet as essential as buying underwear) for the last time.

For years the old woman in the framed photo I bought at a yard sale has watched me from her place on my kitchen wall, with one hand cupping her chin and her eyes seeming to take in simply everything, not missing a single move I've made, yet today a friend who saw the photo recognized the woman and said, "That's Helen Keller."

The alchemist was disappointed when he learned that the philosopher's stone he'd sought his whole life was not one object but *everything*—every object in creation, great and small—but then he learned to laugh about this, and if you listen carefully, you can still sort of hear that laughter.

THE CIARDI

On noticing my copy of Dante's *Inferno,* my father said, "So the translator's John Ciardi, well, how about *that,* it's my friend John, we play poker together every Wednesday," and I said, "Dad, you must mean a different John Ciardi, because *this* guy's a scholar, a *Dante* scholar, so, no offense, he'd never deign to hang out with a boozing, gambling, non-literary type like you," but it turned out that the old man was right—his Ciardi was *the* Ciardi—"*and,*" said my father, "you should hear what a foul mouth John has when he's drunk and on his knees shooting craps on our kitchen floor."

ROCK 'N' ROLL HERNIA (3)

"Should I take a shower before we go to lunch?" asks your friend, the Kabbalah-savvy rock star Benny Pompa, and because you're all for personal hygiene, you say, "Of course," but after contemplating the matter, Benny shakes his head, saying, "Water's overrated, though I guess we all like to *drink* it, at least a little," and then he just walks out of his hotel suite, still pajama-clad and barefoot and expecting you to follow, which you do.

LET'S DRESS LIKE MINNIE PEARL

It was a winter night in Salt Lake City, dear V., and I'd lost my high-rise hotel—the thing had simply vanished since I'd last been there, which was at noon, and only after three drives around the block in my rental car did I realize that the hotel *was* still there but looked invisible because it was blacked-out, darker than dark, which the night manager explained to me (once I'd parked my car and pounded on the entrance) as "a building-wide power loss, *and*," he added, "since the elevators aren't working, I'll have to lead you up the stairwell with a flashlight," which he did, but once we'd climbed eighteen floors on foot, he realized he'd forgotten the special key he'd need to let me in my room, so he said, "Please just wait here while I go down to get that key and then come back," and as soon as I stretched out on the stairwell's concrete steps, the light from his flashlight disappeared, and then the sound of his footsteps disappeared, too, and I understood that I was now in deeper darkness, and deeper silence, than I'd ever known before, which made me feel so desolate until your image came to mind, V., I could visualize you clearly, you a stranger I wouldn't meet for many years yet but still you shone as bright as morning, and I could hear percussive sounds, joyous percussion, because I sensed that when we'd finally meet you would turn my solitary heart into a drum.

HERE AT THE FRIED LIVER WASH

At table eight here at the Fried Liver Wash Café in Sydney, a boy who's been ignored by his parents, called stupid by his teachers, bullied by his schoolmates, and spurned by the girl he loves sits poring over a scroll he swiped from a bookmobile, a scroll entitled, "*Anthology of Precious Secrets on How to Make Gold Dust from Bran.*"

While you sit smoking at table nine, a red-haired guy in a green sweater keeps walking by you to the men's room, sometimes aiming hostile looks in your direction and at other times smiling warmly—an inconsistency you find confusing until you leave the bar, go past his outdoor table, and discover that this one-man good cop/bad cop act is really a pair of identical twins with the same fashion sense.

At table twelve, a woman writes in her diary, "*I've experienced many things that taught me what it means to be human—romantic commitment, homosexual dabbling, learning a foreign language, drug addiction, raising a child, professional success, professional failure, waking up from a drunken rampage to find a baffling new tattoo on my arm, and witnessing the fabled 'green flash' at sunset—but I've never done the one thing that would probably teach me the most: namely, taking another person's life.*"

THEY'LL HAVE TO CATCH US FIRST

Because a taxi driver named Drupka Kemeny sped up to run a red light at the corner of Sixty-Third and Fifth and caused an accident which left him unhurt but killed his passenger, my cousin Maggie, I vowed revenge and staked out Kemeny's home in Queens, but I kept dithering, Hamlet-style, so in the end I left that cousin-killer alone, and now I just tell taxi drivers whenever they're speeding, "Please slow this cab down, I get car-sick," a falsehood that keeps me safe and calms my nerves except one man, on hearing it, slowed his taxi to a crawl, and when I said, "Hey, you don't need to drive this slow," the cabbie said, "Oh, yes, I do, or else you'll puke in my back seat," so on we rolled at five or six miles per hour, and I laughed—how could I not?—when we went creeping by that fatal corner of Sixty-Third and Fifth.

THE JUMBLY BOY

Map began to view his childhood in a new light the day he volunteered for a therapy experiment where trained actors portrayed his family and subjected him to hours of psychodrama, after which he was asked to select the relatives he felt safest with and, despite how poorly his parents always treated him, Map amazed himself by choosing them.

Pryna stopped worrying so much about what people think of her the night she read an interview with Jodorowsky in which he said about his film *El Topo*, "If you're great, then *El Topo* is a great picture; if you're limited, then *El Topo* is limited"—but what truly sealed the deal was Pryna's dream later that night, during which the wizard Merlin told her, "Only fools want to be great."

ZAKHOR (WHAT YOU GAVE)

That time you tried to make me happy by bringing me to meet my favorite wrestler at what we thought was his home near Phoenix but a weeping woman at the door said, "I'm so sorry, no wrestlers live here"; and then that time after you died when I lay on my bed and whispered, "Show me a sign, Ma," and right away this gift from you, a poster of *Christina's World*, peeled off the wall and settled on me like a blanket; and all the times when you'd assure me, "It's just my bad back, don't worry, sweetheart, I won't go dying on you, I promise," but you *were* dying and you knew it, and only years after your death did I come across your letter, the one that said in your handwriting what you couldn't bear to tell me out loud—yes, all those times we spent together you gave and gave and gave and gave, giving all that you were able, I know this now.

SWEET LEAF

Call it a miracle, how this thin, curved orange leaf danced in mid-air for fifteen minutes—autumn had plucked it from a tree branch before gravity took over, but then a strong wind had its say, too, bouncing the leaf around in this surprise of a wild new life—until the wind, fickle as ever, moved on and now the leaf joined its dead brethren on the ground, where they all looked alike.

SHAKE HANDS WITH LIPPY

Just as Marcel Duchamp filled a suitcase with miniature reproductions of his best paintings and sculptures so that when someone asked what kind of artist he was, he could open the suitcase and show them, I want to fill a suitcase with holographic reproductions of my life's most joyous moments (the time my six-year-old son and I danced in a park singing "Kung Fu Fighting," for instance; or the time when my uncle chased me all around his apartment, the two of us laughing our heads off; or the time when my wife and I spun a Wheel of Fortune together), and then, if someone asks me what kind of person I am, I can open my suitcase and show them these memories and say, "For the most part, fucking *blessed.*"

THE LAST LIVING PICTISH SPEAKER
ON THE PLANET

Trisana Braxi was born in 1932 to a butcher father and a bookkeeper mother in the New Jersey town of Short Hills, where she mastered the piano compositions of Debussy and Ravel and then—swearing off all romantic entanglements and borrowing her motto from William Blake: "The Angel that presided o'er my birth / Said, 'Little creature, form'd of Joy and Mirth, / 'Go love without the help of any Thing on Earth'"—Trisana set forth on a lifetime of adventures, which included:

learning to read and write and converse in the Pictish tongue from its last living speaker, a woman known as Miss Hale (who was a descendent of the American Revolution's young martyr Nathan Hale);

stealing for a rich collector a noted anti-Theosophy tract entitled *I Knew Madame Blavatsky When She Was Sweet Sixteen*;

dreaming a lovely dream in which people for some reason kept calling her "Ethel";

gluing a photo of herself on the ceiling above her bed so that every morning when Trisana woke up she could say, "*You* again!";

sleeping with a Jamaican man who banged a gong beside his own bed whenever he gave Trisana an orgasm;

working as a deep-sea diver, which allowed her to swim near vampire squids, fire-breathing shrimp, giant larvaceans living in clouds of mucous, and anglerfish with lightbulbs dangling from their foreheads;

discovering in the restroom of an Esso station in Annandale-on-Hudson a sea-chest containing pieces of eight, enough of them to finance her lifetime of adventures;

feeling insulted when a drunk man at a Dodgers game told her, "Hey, babe, I like you—but then again, I like Newark";

leaning in a doorway in Old Jerusalem when a tour guide pointed to her and told his group, "This woman is standing on one of the spots where Jesus rested during his forced walk to Golgotha";

entering, on a lark, a beauty contest at Coney Island and taking second place as the 1954 "Pastrami Queen";

surviving leprosy in Malaysia, beriberi in Sicily, scurvy in Alexandria, bubonic plague in Persia, pellagra in Madagascar, an earthquake in Japan, a shipwreck in the Strait of Magellan, and a respiratory ailment, which she cured by riding on top of the "City of New Orleans" train with her mouth constantly held open to let the purifying air in;

receiving a dollar bill on which someone had scrawled in a balloon coming from George Washington's mouth the phrase "I Grew Hemp";

feeling lonely sometimes, and missing her butcher father, and questioning her life choices yet still maintaining her good figure by adhering daily to the "Little Rascals Diet" (a wedge of Limburger cheese, some toast smeared with mush, and a teaspoon of castor oil);

traveling around the Pacific Northwest in the company of a crusty old woman named Vernita Wheat, who liked to say, "I'm different from regular people—I drink from the Great Mother's breasts";

visiting with Vernita "the Big Rock Candy Mountain," where they enjoyed the cigarette trees, paper money–laden bushes, lakes made of whiskey and stew, plus jails easily escaped from;

feeling guilty about stealing that tract about Madame Blavatsky until she stole it back and returned it to its rightful owner;

experiencing what she, Trisana, would call her "Copenhagen Epiphany" while seated in a café in that city ("*A beam of light struck a clear glass teacup at the table next to mine and suddenly a profound peace descended on me, and I realized that everything which happened in my past had been exactly as it should have been, just as everything that would happen in my future would be exactly as it should be*—everything in its right place—*and this epiphany might have gone on, too, but the waitress there interrupted it by asking me if I wanted more tea*");

savoring the best pickup-line-at-a-cocktail-party she'd ever heard: "Kiss me, I'm mortal";

writing fond letters to her butcher father but diplomatically ignoring his entreaties for her to come home;

ignoring, too, a bank check that arrived in her PO box, a check made out in zeroes and signed by "*Dethe Thee Great Levyller Who Comes To Alle Menne*";

enjoying an erotic evening with two chaps named Gog and Magog;

realizing, on learning of Miss Hale's death, that she, Trisana, was now the last living Pictish speaker on the planet;

spending time in a Trader Vic's with a Thompson gun-wielding mercenary named Roland and hearing of his mentor Hassan ibn Sabbah, the "Old Man of the Mountain," who founded the hashish-eating Assassins sect and who always said, "Nothing is true, everything is permitted";

falling into a game pit while exploring a jungle in Vietnam but getting saved from its mud-caked wooden stakes by her guide, a reformed cannibal with very white teeth;

legally changing her name to "Rain Sabitrax" (an anagram of "Trisana Braxi") after learning of a Talmudic tradition in which someone will assume a new monicker so that the Angel of Death can never find them;

legally changing her name back to "Trisana Braxi" after learning of a Taoist tradition in which the Heavenly Bureaucracy will bestow good fortune on anyone who stays faithful, no matter what, to who they truly are;

visiting Estonia on the very day that the nation's new currency was issued, which meant that everyone except for Trisana walked around staring in wonder at the colored paper rectangles in their hands;

standing in line outside a movie theater reading a magazine interview with the magician Ricky Jay and getting to the part where Jay talks about what coincidences truly mean right when Jay himself walked up to stand behind Pryna, intent on seeing the same film;

still feeling lonely sometimes, and missing her butcher father, and questioning her life choices while trying to live by the maxim "Don't gloat when you win or whine when you lose" (and interrupting anyone who whines by snapping at them, "Tell it to Anne Frank");

finding a bottle labeled "Sweat from the Body of a Just-Hanged Man" in a new friend's pantry and high-tailing out of there before the dinner bell;

laughing at a drunk man at a Knicks game who told her, "Hey, hon, I like you—but then again, I like hemorrhoids";

having a terrific time at a Chicago art gallery opening where the all-too-human-looking guests, unbeknownst to Trisana, were Hotei, the Japanese god of abundance, Santoshi Mata, the Hindu "Mother of Satisfaction," Oshua, the Yoruban deity of sweetness, Fufluns, the Etruscan god of springtime, and Fulushou, the Chinese trinity of joy;

arm-wrestling Lilith Blueskiller to a verified draw in a Key West bar called "Hog's Breath," where the cocktail coasters read, *"Hog's Breath Is Better Than No Breath At All"*;

learning how to make "cowboy coffee" and how to play "cowboy guitar chords" from Schlepin' Bob Lariott, who also taught her how to sing "Streets of Laredo," "San Francisco Bay Blues," and "Your Sweet and Shiny Eyes";

watching while bound in chains as the pirate captain Seven Seas Jim was made to walk the plank of his own ship, *La Sylphyde*, by his mutinous crew;

gazing in awe at a big public clock in Paris whose hands, due to a malfunction, raced backward in time, faster and faster, until Trisana felt out of breath;

asking for the blessing of Solomon Fern, a wizened centenarian she met at a shuffleboard contest, and receiving that blessing, sort of ("*I was hoping for a fancy ritual, where he would lay his hands on my head and invoke the gods, but all he did was say,* 'Don't smoke tobacco'");

hiking through the Gobi Desert by following a trail of bones, camel droppings, glittery shards from a meteorite, discarded calabashes of sour curds, and the mirage-image of a child named Gary;

sitting in with a jazz band in Budapest and playing "My Funny Valentine" on a piano much like her own back in New Jersey;

learning the concept of *amor fati* when she encountered the Three Fates with their wooden loom set up and spinning on a Fort Lauderdale sidewalk ("*I asked one of them—Clotho, Lachesis, or Atropos, I'm not sure which—when death could come for me, and she said, 'We never divulge such data, not even to our relatives, but in the meantime, dearie, we advise you to learn to love your fate'*");

winning a Pawnee show-coat made of pressed buffalo hide while playing a game of *Risk* with more accomplished players;

beginning to fall in love with Prester Jeanne, the female monarch of a hidden African kingdom, but fleeing Jeanne's palace under cover of night because Trisana feared she'd break her to vow to herself about avoiding all romantic entanglements;

making a new vow, as she strolled through a valley in
Tanzania, that she would enjoy her travels from now on not only
for herself but also for the spirit of her butcher father, who had
died the previous year and who would have loved this place;

politely refusing offers of tobacco wherever she went;

whistling "Georgy Girl," her all-time favorite pop song, while
pondering Violet Weingarten's evergreen question "Is life too
short to be taking shit, or is life too short to be minding it?";

speaking of questions, asking the ghost of Rabbi Low why he
wasn't able to build a golem to fight the Nazis in Europe;

acting as an extra in a movie with the up-and-coming
Hollywood starlet Sharon Tate;

scattering flowers at the feet of a magus, Fuikksho Shimamoto,
who told her that in another world her name was Ethel and that
this Ethel-incarnation of Trisana was living a far less fulfilled life
and would die of cancer before turning fifty;

receiving a gift of Holy Grail earrings from a tambourine-
shaking, football-flinging old hippie named Gypsy Boots in a
Gordita Beach hotel lobby;

disco-dancing at *Nave Jungla*, a most unusual Buenos Aires
nightclub, with a young painter named Raul and his boyfriend;

ignoring a second bank check that arrived in her PO box,
a check made out in zeroes and signed by *"Dethe Thee Great
Levyller Who Comes To Alle Menne"*;

enjoying an erotic evening with two chaps named Jack-of-
Green and Jack-in-Irons, though for most of it she fantasized
about Prester Jeanne, who, unbeknownst to Trisana, was at that
moment fantasizing about her;

receiving another dollar bill with George Washington saying,
"I Grew Hemp" and wondering if this was the same such bill that
had passed through her fingers so many moons ago;

forgetting a word in Pictish and worrying that, by the time she died, she'd have forgotten many more of them, if not all;

gazing at the Winter Palace in Saint Petersburg as a Russian friend explained, "The sight of this building gave us hope against the Soviets, it said a silent *nyet* to them, because we knew that if such human-made beauty existed here once, then maybe someday it would again";

meeting a man named Marvin and laughing when he told her that he'd won first place as "Kishke King" at the same 1954 Coney Island beauty contest where Trisana took second place as "Pastrami Queen";

laughing some more when Marvin told her, "God has lousy penmanship—did he write across this universe 'I am now here' or 'I am nowhere?'";

reclining on the Pont Neuf in Paris when a tour guide pointed to her and told his group, "This woman is sitting on the exact spot where Jacques de Molay, the last Grand Master of the Knights Templar, was burned at the stake in 1314";

befriending a wanderer who never left New York because she said she hadn't finished exploring Bryant Park yet, and a poet named Yao Fu who began and finished each poem by writing, "Yao Fu does not write poems just for fun," and a dancer who hung his top hat on a sun ray in the alley where the 1930s bank robber John Dillinger got gunned down;

fretting about turning fifty until the artist Captain Beefheart told her, "Just take the five, straighten it out, and use it to spear the shit out of the zero";

getting past the velvet rope at Xenon (Studio 54's biggest competitor) because the bouncer there grinned at the sight of Trisana's yin-yang necklace and said, "Hey, *you're* balanced, go on in!";

viewing a double rainbow in the sky over Richmond while licking a strawberry ice-cream cone that she'd purchased at a store called "Double Rainbow";

agreeing with a writer named Tom McGuane when he told her, "America has become a dildo that's turned berserkly on its owner" and wishing she could build a golem strong enough to fight the new Nazis in her homeland;

hearing pieces by Debussy and Ravel at a piano bar in Bangkok and feeling how odd it was that she'd grown old while this music she'd first loved as a child had stayed the same;

writing a book about her friends and family and lovers, a book with the working title "We Love the World And Plan to Stay";

meeting her alter ego Ethel in a sweet dream and taking Ethel's hands in hers as Trisana told her, "In another world, sister, a *better* world, we could meet and drink from the Great Mother's breasts together";

weeping for her butcher father on the ferry from Hong Kong to Kowloon as someone near her sang the Seekers' song "I'll Never Find Another You";

and finally, influenced by the feelings stirred up by this ferry ride, moving back into her dead parents' home in New Jersey, where she married that guy named Marvin, the Coney Island–crowned "Kishke King," and gave birth, despite her advanced age, to a boy named Gary, and now she's teaching them how to read and write and speak Pictish, whatever of it she still remembers, and when "Dethe Thee Great Levyller Who Comes To Alle Menne" comes to her, Trisana Braxi feels certain that dying will feel much like her "Copenhagen Epiphany," the reason for this certainty being that she has learned to love her fate.

GOODBYE, MY BOOK!

"I write stories that are only one sentence long," I explain to you as I plant this book like a time bomb in your public library, "because imperfection is easier to tolerate in small doses."

MOONBURN: THE SEQUEL

You woke to find the full moon on your cheek, neatly balanced as if it belonged there, but before you could mistake it for something else, it turned into a firefly and flew home, giving off enough light for you to know it.

"ALS ICH KAN"

ACKNOWLEDGMENTS

For professional support, I warmly thank Tyson Cornell, Guy Intoci, and Hailie Johnson at Rare Bird Books. Thanks as well to my pal, the terrific Internet wizard Fotis Tzanakis (great call, Laura Albert!)—and to Linh Dinh, whose one-sentence stories in his fine collection *Blood and Soap* lit the spark.

I'm also immensely grateful to the aforementioned Ms. Albert, David Amram, Laurie Anderson, David "Bomba" Baum, Lorraine Bracco, Sarah Bloom, Tamara Braun, Carla Capretto, Chris Cardy, Nathalie Detourne, Marvin Dunn, Barry Ellsworth, Rosie Flores, Carolyn "MG" Garcia, Juan Guzman, Yasmine Hamdan, Carol Huang, Kimberly Huie, Eugene Hutz and Victoria Espinosa, Michael Hyde, Michael and Victoria Imperioli, Heidi James, Charles and Susan and Josh Kalish, Dorka Keehn, David and Suzanne Keil, Rick and Bev Kestenbaum, Simon and Maria Angelica Kirke, Ilene Landress, Jillian Lauren, the Lippmans (Suzanne, Ben, David, Linds, Beth, Steve, and Jacki), Steve List, Dave Lombardi, Pam Lubell and (my coolest reader) James Hammond, Lydia Lunch, Paula Madrid, Ann Marlowe, Patricia Marx, Dana McCoy, Sergio and Susana Medina, Bob Neuwirth, Jimbo Ospenson and Meryl Perlman, Myra Pasek, Melodie Provenzano, Natalia Repolovsky, Matthew Rhys and Keri Russell, Nic Richard and Julie Bonnie, Lou Rittmaster, Tom Robbins, Maria and Lori Santoro, Yvette Scharf, Susan Schreiber, Tammy Jo Setner, Larry "Ratso" Sloman, the Smiths (Richard, Martin and David), Jeff Stein, Sara Sugarman, Sean Sullivan, Haviva, Eve and Joshua Swirsky, Jacques Thelemaque, Maureen and Stevie Van Zandt, Andres Virkus and Margy Rung, Judith Weinstein, Michael Wherly, Jonathan Young and Audrey Grumhaus, as well as my goddaughters Thelma and Lorelye.

Where would I be without L. Gabrielle Penabaz, Stacey Bell, Eileen Salzig, Brigitte Bako, Bill Ehrlich, Larry Kirstein, Arnie Civins, Sean Fellin, Matt Marcello, Alan Dreher, Michael Bush, Antony Wong, Mariela Rosales, and the ever-amazing Cathy Clarke, whose help with this book was invaluable?

Very much missed are Bobby Lippman, Frau Elisabeth Schmeding, Madeleine Jensen, Irving Cooperberg, Ole Egset, Harry Crews, Gypsy Boots, John Perry Barlow, Kevin Byrd, Maryellen Cataneo, Ceil and Norman, Ian Cuttler, Jack Garfein, Wendell Green, Michael Greene, Amie Harwick, Nina Mattson, Meg Mazursky, Daniel Menaker, T-Shirt Philippe, Lou Reed, Lisa Roy, Sarah Rubin, Marla Ruzicka, Sam and Mildred Schreiber, Rona Smith, Scott Sommer, Hal Willner, and Ida Winston.

Thanks as well to Tatiana Abbey, Masha Alloin, Alosha and Vali, Scott Asen, Norena Barbella, Joan Juliet Buck, Dan and Beth Bootzin, Richard Bradley, David Brendel, Arthur Cacossa, Anne Chang, Vin Cycz, Huy Dao, the Delaney/McCarthy/Collinson trio, Michael Des Barres, Janine DiGiovani, Linda Dinerstein, Pam Esterson, Hampton Fancher, Sharyn Felder and Will, JuliJo Fehrle, Danny Fields, Rachel Fox, Ray Gange, Debra Ginsberg, Adriane Glazier, Bobby and Kathy Golden, Roi Gonen, Adam Grosso, Rajesh Gulab, Maite Iracheta, Angela Janklow, Kees van V., Danny "Kootch" Kortchmar, Steve Krulwich, Scott Shriner, Susan Lehman, Diana Lehr, Gary Lucas, Maryellen Matthews, Mert and Defne, Monroe and Danvy, Jenna Moskowitz, Maria and Jenni Muldaur, Mark Murphy, Nadine Neema, Willie Nile and Cris, May Pang, Barbara Petratos, Pippin Petty-Schroeppel, Pat Place, Keith Raywood, Derrick Rossi, Eric Sandys, Jessica Schwartz, Dan Seligman, George Sheanshang, Christy Smith, Dalia Sofer, Jerry Stahl, Jeff Stettin, Chris Davis, Supercali, Magic Carla and Alex, Russ Titelman, Holly Troy, Monica Vaughan, Ali Zacker, George

Zaver, Zsofi Tomasz, Sandrine Bluet, Vanessa Potkin, Hans Chew, Txiki Margalef, and Elizabeth Kipp-Guisti, plus anyone I forgot.

Cool quotes from Jonathan Young, Auden, Burroughs, Chesterton, Garcia Marquez, Kevin Ayers, Leonard Cohen, Loren Eiseley, Roky Erickson, Jim Harrison, Irryku, R.A. Lafferty, Stephen Mitchell, Thomas McGuane, Iggy Pop, Manuel Puig, Tom Robbins, Arnold Rothstein, Wislawa Szymborska, James Thurber, Eliot Weinberger, the Dead Milkmen, and that kid at EJs.

Let me hereby declare my love to Ethel Lippman ("from here to the moon and back 100 million times"), Bernard Lippman (Charlie Samsam says hi), David and Lena (Lily) Fern, David and Lena (Lulu) Lippman, my lovely co-parent Ingunn Egset, Prester John Bliss, Szombathelyi Marika and Istvan (the glorious parents I dreamed of and finally found), Szilard (Dr. Meyer) and Ginger, my dear Norma Lippman, and the fabulous fjord-dwelling Bodil and Ols Egset.

Even if I had my pick to parent any child in the universe, I'd go with my son Gabriel Olai Beauregard Egset, whose wit, warmth, resilience, and brilliance "make me feel ten feet tall."

If I owe my sanity—indeed, my existence—to a single person, it's my uncle Dr. William H. Fern, who for nearly six decades has listened to me vent, helped me to "tailor expectations," shared family lessons, imbued me with his courage, served as my greatest teacher, and has enhanced the lives of hundreds of other people.

Finally, this book (and I myself) would not exist if not for the flower of Veszprem, my wife Szombathelyi Vera Kata, a tender, wise, beautiful, and fun soul who's given me a loving home while helping me to "grow up" and acting as my first and best reader, for which I say "*Szeretlek nagyon big-time*" to you, *Mutyi*...

You're the top, kids. Let's meet in Taumatawhakatangihang-akoauauotamateaturipukakapikimaungahoronukupokaiwhenua-kitanatahu!